Scoundrel

a male/male romance by

Wendy Rathbone

Antares is a willing sex slave, trained in the harems of Anada since the age of 18, and owned by a wealthy master who spoils his slaves. But all that changes when Empire soldiers invade Antares' world and he is taken away from the only life he's ever known.

In a colonized galaxy where starships are as common as houseflies, and a dark Empire seeks to control thousands of civilized worlds, there are those who fall through the cracks and refuse to be conquered, including the pirate, Slate, and his crew.

Out in the darkness of the unknown, among Empire soldiers and scoundrels, will bad fates befall Antares and his fellow captive companions?

Will Slate finally find the love he's been looking for his whole life?

Can Slate and Antares ever see eye to eye?

A male/male romance to end all male/male romances!

<u>Dedication</u>

*For Della, for her editing skills
and all she does for me*

and

*Christina E. Pilz
for her insightful comments
and suggestions*

Scoundrel

Prologue

Made of stardust and mercury and the whispers of Bridge World winds.

I read the words on the ad copy the ship's former sales rep had prepared. I never would have seen the ad, nor would I be telling this story now if this starship hadn't been hijacked months ago en route to the barbaric fringe planets of Sector 818.

The words were lies, of course.

My name is Antares. I and my companions aboard this ship were born like any other mammalian beings, and were comprised of many races and colors. Sure, at age eighteen, when I consented to be trained in the arts of pleasure, my DNA had been altered to give off a honeyed scent. The texture of my skin was satin to the touch, and my libido enhanced. But I was no more or less made of mercury than any other human. But we're all part stardust, or so they say. It is where we come from and where we will some day return.

I am writing my story in a book of ice given to me by a thief from a planet burnt by a thousand year war. The ice is preserved by a tiny stasis field forming the book's crystal clear cover. The pages are thin, unlined parchments made from several ingredients, including powdered quartz.

On any market, legitimate or black, it would cost a fortune. But it cost him nothing. For he is a thief of great skill and infamy.

When I touch the book I can feel tiny vibrations from the stasis field. It is always cool but not freezing.

I long to write words so fiery and furious they might melt the very bindings that hold this book together.

When I tell you my story, we'll see what happens.

I call this my journal of fire and ice.

Chapter One

From childhood on we were told: *The world of Anada is a rose. It blooms everywhere, even in the weeds, through the darkness and the trash. The blue roads of Anada lead to the stars and, if you travel long enough and far, you will be able to touch them.*

I had touched flowers plenty, but never touched stars. Until the war came.

The first time I saw Anada from space, I looked upon a teal-jade jewel floating in impossible blackness. It was not a rose, but it was still beautiful. There were no blue roads, though, and I was leaving the beauty, safety and peace of my home planet forever.

My last view of it was marred by ships crossing that watery green orb, dark wing-shaped things like locusts closing in to cloud all light, to descend, to rend, to feed.

The Empire war had reached us. The starguard's billion lightyear march. We were but victims on their long journey of destruction and terrible reign.

At three in the afternoon, a warm, breezy day filled with blue skies and crisp scents, the burning tang of the Empire's fleet began to edge the air. We knew they were coming. We waited and did nothing.

It was over before it even started. We are a peaceful people. We didn't fight.

They took me and my kind away first. The pleasure slaves.

I don't know what happened to the rest of my people. Killed, no doubt, or taken prisoner and kept planet-side as long as they remained non-combative. They would be indoctrinated to serve the new regime. Obey their laws. Recite their policies. Join their armies. Fight their fight.

We pleasure slaves were rounded up and separated into a thousand different groups. We were a valued commodity. We'd be auctioned off for funds to further the war effort.

I was shoved with 29 others into a shuttle. Of those 29, I personally knew four: Ocean, Amethyst, Dusk, and Nile. The others I had never met or seen before.

We formed a line and took our assigned seats as metal-garbed soldiers watched us with dead, dry eyes through slits in their face-masks. We were not given clothes. We were fed only small amounts of water and food at various intervals. They did not take our jewels or other embellishments, which in itself seemed strange, but maybe they would be sold with us as "part of the package."

I wore an emerald studded belt that rode my hips and accentuated my flat belly. Two leather strips, one in front and one in back, joined between my legs in a ring through which my cock and balls protruded. The ring was silver with tiny diamonds embedded in it.

On my wrists were two matching silver bracelet cuffs glinting with tiny rainbowed stones. I had two rings on each hand: one emerald, one ruby, two sapphires. A necklace glinted from my smooth, hairless chest, a silver triangle with inlaid mermaid scales.

My owner had been a rich man and he liked the three slaves he kept—me, Ocean, and Amethyst—to be always adorned with precious gems and alloys. We all had long hair—mine in dark gold curls hanging just below my nipples—with gemstones braided into that as well.

And that was it. No scarves, no loincloths, no shoes or slippers. We were shipped in this way, naked and afraid, male and female alike, to be sold away from the safety and pleasure of our realm, all of us knowing our fortunes had turned evil.

On Anada, for more than twenty generations of pleasure slavery, the rules of the harems where we were trained and, later, the homes where we lived, kept us healthy and happy. In the Empire that knew no such rules, we would be subject to individual whim, or insanity. As objects of the Empire, not real citizens with any right to a voice, we might be abused or destroyed as our owners pleased.

Our shuttle docked to one of the starships waiting against the ever-wheeling welkin of stars. The starguards herded us into the docking bay and into an adjoining cargo bay with stripes of yellow light across the ceiling, a hard floor strewn with 30 mattresses, and a few hard benches along one bulkhead.

The room was not cold, but we were all shivering. Most of us had tear-smudged faces, and on many the tears still flowed. I had not yet cried. Everything felt stopped up at the back of my throat, all my feelings, all my fears. I thought if I opened my mouth to speak I would surely choke.

Several of the guards, behind their frightening armored masks, laughed at us. The masks were actually part of their helmets, dull gray with dark edges where they swept over the eyes and nose for protection. The holes for the eyes were slits and made them look like half-drawn creatures awaiting completion. We could not see their faces, their emotions. Their soulless demeanors and hard shells made them purposely intimidating, even though we logically knew there were humans beneath the armor.

At the door, three guards seemed to be conferring. After a minute, two came toward Amethyst and me. One guard raised his hand and touched Amethyst's full, left breast where small red jewels had been glued around the nipple. She stood quite still, used to being admired, but her eyes were wide and wet. She had been admired by friends, grooms, lovers and owners. Never monster conquerors from the stars. She shivered at his caress.

The other guard simply grabbed my upper arm and pulled me forward.

Amethyst and I were led from the room, leaving the others behind.

Chapter Two

The three starguards took us quickly through the docking bay. The area contained four shuttles. Mechanics crawled over their surfaces like vermin, working. Starguards stood in various spots around the massive deck. We passed close by two of them as we approached a door. One muttered under his breath, "Not supposed to play with the merchandise."

The guard who trailed behind us turned and, out the corner of my eye, I saw him quickly belt the door guard, who slammed up against the bulkhead with an ugly, clanking sound. It couldn't have hurt; he was too thickly armored.

"Hey," he squealed. "I was just sayin'."

Our guard said, "You can join us or shut up."

He stayed in his position, shaking his masked head. The other door guard remained silent, but his head tilted up and down as if he were laughing.

We went through the door otherwise un-accosted, and into a white corridor. At the end of the corridor stood an open door that led to a room with plush, beige couches, tables and what looked like a kitchen off to the side. A small rec room, or lunch room, I surmised.

The trailing guard closed the door and pushed a button. I could hear an internal lock set in place.

The room had a sort of diffused pink light and smelled a bit of processed air and peanut butter. Three couches made a 'U' in the middle of the room. At the kitchen area stood a table with about ten chairs surrounding it. The bulkheads were white, the furniture new but drab, off-white and gray, and the kitchen and its appliances were silver, gray and white.

Nothing remarkable or of note except one thing. The starfield that made up the furthest wall. That one wall was a two-way monitor, a window to space. And the stars shone there like a mist upon the great black beyond.

I had been surrounded by beauty all my life, but never this. My first time off-world, I was in fear and amazement combined. And I realized for the first time how big it all was and how I, a spoiled, pampered boy who thrived on pleasure, was nothing amid all of that.

I froze, gawking. The blockage in my throat, my pent up feelings, my terror, all my wonder increased. I opened my mouth. Exhaled. Everything seemed to stop. I stared and felt my skin lift from itself a little, my blood speed up. If I did not live another second, I thought, well, I had seen this. I was less than a speck before it all, and yet in my abject grief my soul felt grand, as if it had met its origin. There was no end. Just timlessness. Forever. And me here now with the gift of existence to be a part of it if only for a moment, at one with a fleeting season called life.

My stomach rippled. My leg muscles, my buttocks, my back. It felt a little like falling, this new scene.

"Hey." A tug at my arm.

It took me some seconds to notice the starguard at my side trying to yank me toward one of the couches.

Another voice said, "He's a space virgin. Isn't that cute. Acts like he's never seen stars before."

I blinked. The room and the guards came into focus again. And all the blurry grayness of their armor, the décor, the color of wartime, loss, nothing.

I inhaled sharply, turning so abruptly the guard startled and smacked me on the chest, sending me sprawling onto the nearest couch.

Only then did I realize the other two men already had Amethyst down on the couch. Their helmets were off, revealing two young, gruff men, one with brown skin, one pink-faced and pale. Their gloves littered the floor. They had already pushed her legs apart and were examining her as if they'd never seen a girl before, stroking the lips of her genitals, spreading them, dipping their fingers into her.

She was so pretty down there, the plump vaginal lips red and shiny, hairless as we all were made immediately upon being taking into training. She could not help but love the attention, even if it was unasked for or unwarranted. Our libidos ran high. We needed touch, craved it. It was our job. The chosen focus of our lives.

What we didn't want was to be hurt. We knew the pleasures of spankings and light whippings, but always in a safe space where we had attention and comfort when needed, and instant grooming and salves and potions from servants if necessary.

But this was our gift. Pleasure. In pretty much any form. We ruled here. We were unsurpassed in our art; we were that well-trained.

Amethyst was saying to the two attentive men, "I accept your pleasures, both of you. You may look at me, caress me, taste me, fuck me as you wish, just please don't hurt us, any of us, please."

The pale man laughed. "We'll do as we want." He slapped her breast.

She was used to roughness, well-trained. She did not recoil. She merely smiled through her shock and lifted herself up on the couch, hands under her buttocks, to entice them further so they would forget about being the bullies they were.

As I said, we ruled in this arena. Not just physically, but psychologically as well.

They both stroked her again between her legs, marveling at her soft richness, her wet beckonings. Their fingers spread her. One lowered his head and licked with a probing tongue into her, then pursed his lips as if trying to drink from her.

12

Our owner had called Amethyst his lily. He said she tasted of flowers and sugar. She bloomed like a flower for him as many times a day as he wanted her. She fed him her internal elixirs, which never ran dry, until it seemed her vagina sucked at his mouth instead of the reverse, and she took his cock into her with the ease of a breath.

How he had loved her.

He had loved me and Ocean, too, for the different things we could do with him and for him, but Amethyst was his favorite.

She once told me she came nine times in one session. I couldn't fathom it, even with my own enhanced libido. She was master of her art.

Now she coaxed the two men into taking off all their armor and the underclothes beneath it. She stroked their naked hips. She sucked them hard in minutes, her long, dark hair playing over their cocks as her strong mouth worked them. Then she invited the bigger of the two to plunder her while she continued to suck the other.

For now, a terrible situation was temporarily under control.

My own guard had been watching them as intently as I. Now he turned to me, removing his helmet. He had dark brown hair and green eyes. He was not as ugly as Amethyst's two, but still maybe a little too young for my tastes. I liked them marinated a little, seasoned. This one's cheeks were a little too fat for his face, but his curiosity hooked me. I was ready to please him, and no longer afraid in this moment. In fact, with everything that had happened to us these past few days, I found it a relief to be distracted in this way.

I loved men. There was a richness to them, a heat in the blood that was undeniably arousing to me, a scent, a texture. And of course the majesty and warmth of the cock. I had been aroused just by looking at penises since I was a boy and probably should not have thought such things, but that was the way of it for me. In the bisexual culture of Anada it didn't matter. You could prefer whomever you wished, though we were raised to want it all.

Slowly, my guard traced my cock with two fingers, up and down, and just the touch sent tingles throughout my body. My libido never slept. I saw his eyes looking at the belt, trying to figure it out. He asked, touching the ring, "Does this hurt?"

"No."

I could hear the fucking on the other couch, the liquid gliding of mouth and genitals that made slurping sounds, the grunts and groans, Amethyst's erotically-whispered encouragements when she popped the cock from her mouth every once in awhile to milk it with her lovely fingers. If the men were not used to her, they would not last. They'd be coming in moments.

I helped my guy out of his armor, grateful, actually, that I'd been chosen along with Amethyst to accompany these guards. I was away from the hold, away from fear. I could control this situation. For now.

When he was nude I saw he was already erect. I reached out to touch him but he leaned away and asked softly, "May I? First?" He reached for my cock.

"Of course." I had the strange feeling he'd never had a man before and yet had been longing for it.

He stroked me all over my body. "Your skin, what has been done to it? It feels like water, or silk."

"On Anada, we go through a lot of processes before we are sold."

"I have never heard of Anada before we came to conquer it," he admitted. "They have done things to you. You are just so, so beautiful."

"It's on purpose."

Both his palms smoothed over the insides of my thighs. He moved them up, tapped at my bobbing cock, cupped my balls. "May I?" he asked.

I wasn't sure what he was asking for, but my automatic response to anyone sexually was, "Yes."

He then lowered his head and licked the tip of my cock. Licked at the moisture there that was already beginning. I felt his tongue lap me, warm and strong, the texture of it against my glans so soft, giving. A warmth ran all over my body, my skin made of little flames. He grew bolder and sucked in the tip, rolling it on his tongue. Very nice.

Then he sat back.

Strange. I thought this encounter would be different. I thought he would just take me without thought, hump me into the bulkhead until he couldn't stand. But this?

I looked at him. "Would you like me to do that for you?"

His eyes widened. "Yes," he said breathily.

I wondered again. Was this some kind of virgin?

I shoved him back onto the couch with my hand flat on his chest. With my other hand I pushed his legs apart, ran my palm up his thigh and around his hard cock, tickling the pubic hair with my fingers, pulling slightly. Then I took my other hand from his chest and put it underneath his balls, cupping. I leaned down. I lightly licked all along the underside of his cock. Just that. And he groaned and his head fell back onto the arm of the couch. His eyes closed. I had him that easy. Just as Amethyst had her two doing her bidding without them even seeming to notice they weren't the ones in control.

I'd noted that one of her men had already climaxed, the one she had sucked so well. Now he nuzzled at her breast while the other was reaching his own heights of pleasure inside her. If they weren't done after that, she wouldn't care. She would pleasure them for hours if they asked her.

I sucked the head of my guard's cock and he groaned again, louder, pushing up. He was so quickly stiff and ready. How young was he? I let him in further as his hips jerked out of control, sucking him all the way in, feeling the tip against the back of my throat. I could've taken more. Large men were no problem for me.

I pulled back. He was losing control already, I could see. I smiled and went to work on him, using all my talent. When he started yelling, "Oh my god," over and over, the thrill of it hardened me more. It wasn't him that aroused me. It was simply my nature. My art in what I was doing.

I eased my efforts and kept him from coming for another minute, but that was all he was good for. When I knew he couldn't hold back anymore, I sucked hard and fast and he filled my mouth with his liquid, pulsing strong and hard a good ten times.

When he could sit up, he shook the brown bangs from his eyes. "That was amazing!"

"Well, it's supposed to be. But no more of that after now. You conquered my world. There'll be no more of us after we're gone."

He frowned, staring at my still-erect cock. "That's just the way. The weak will always lose."

I did not try to hide my disgust. "So I've been told." I wiggled my hips. My cock bounced slightly. I could tell he wanted to taste more of it. He reached out and wrapped his fingers around it.

I could see on the couch next to us that Amethyst's men were resting, but she was still enticing them, stroking their backs and in between their buttocks, kissing their little budding nipples, letting them lick her again and again as she lifted herself to their mouths. She'd have them going again if they had the time for it.

I didn't know if they all were on a short break or had finished their shifts.

My guy was licking me again, unable to resist my unique scent, my flavor. He said, softly, "I don't think I can take all of you into my mouth."

I pushed back a laugh. "It's okay." I petted his head, guiding him down.

16

He was able, after a little while, to take me in half-way. The play of his tongue was nice. He was unpracticed, but I was used to that. In my harem on Anada before I was sold to my owner, when I was more skilled and had moved onto teaching, the young ones had practiced on me. I loved it all.

When he got bolder, he used his hands on me, then gripped my belt, pulling me forward with it, turning his head, working me. I liked that. In another galaxy, another time, he might've made a good pleasure slave himself.

One of the reasons I was chosen on Anada for pleasure slavery was my sensitivity. It wasn't hard for me to come, but I could also make it last. I had control. I was so easily responsive.

The young guard worked me quite fine even in his inexperience, and I shot heavily into his mouth, making him sputter in surprise even as he came up grinning.

He was already hard again.

I thought about mentioning fucking between men, but he didn't seem to need or want it. So instead I showed him what sixty-nining was about, and had him laughing as he came again.

When the time came to leave, we did not want to part from our thoroughly pleasured guards. As with any pleasure slave, once we got to know a potential owner, even if we didn't particularly care for them, we felt safe with them. They were the "known." Everything else was unknown.

But soon they all had to don their armor and masks. I guess they had another shift.

Amethyst and I shivered as we were led into the white corridor and back to the cargo bay. I was starving and thirsty. None of them had offered us sustenance other than their own bodily fluids.

I hoped there was something to eat back in the hold.

Chapter Three

We had a make-shift kitchen which was too small for 30 people. But we made do. There was water. There were stacks of soup and noodle packs. And vitamins. Nothing fresh. We all shared two bathrooms, one on either end of the hold. They did not contain showers, so all we could manage were spit-baths.

The three guards who initially took Amethyst and me away never returned. Twice a day new guards checked on us, but never remained. They only noted on tablets our supplies in the food area and the two bathrooms.

Some of us were silent and withdrawn, sleeping a lot, sitting alone against the walls or on mattresses.

Others utilized their time to do what they loved and did best. Have sex. They did it out in the open, uninhibited. That was how it had been done in the harems where most of us lived for two years of training before any thought of being sold.

I watched the couplings, sometimes, for lack of anything else to do, and my libido demanded release at least once a day. Nile and Dusk were my favorite pair.

Back when I had trained some of the slaves, before I was adopted by my Anadan owner, I'd helped train Nile. Dusk and Nile were a couple, having attached to each other at an early age before both consented to go into pleasure slavery together at age 18, and they had been put up for adoption as a pair. Their owner and mine were friends, and we had seen each other over the past few years several times a year. It was simple luck that they were in the same group as Ocean, Amethyst and I were in.

Watching Dusk and Nile make love never got old. They were so in love, and so good at it. They would twist around each other and wrap themselves up so tight. Bright and dark they were, one blond with golden skin, the other dark brown. They would merge so fully in their fucking that they almost looked like they were passing right through each other.

Nile had a long uncircumcised cock that was always hard against his taut belly. He was thin and tall, and loved to be sucked for hours on his back, never tiring. Dusk was like his name, dark in coloring, his cock thick and ready, with a pink, shiny knob. They would take turns being on top.

Right now Dusk was putting it to Nile from behind, stroking in and out, his dark cock glistening. Nile's long erection stood up from between his legs. He begged me to come over and suck him. "Antares, come here. Come here!" But I shook my head, staying where I was, my arms folded over my chest, ignoring my own hardness.

Ocean finally went over and took him into his mouth, and Nile went crazy, bucking back and forth, riding Dusk as he thrust into Ocean's mouth. It was amazing. But--

As the days wore on, my enthusiasm had waned. Even for that.

It was less about the idea that my life was over, than it was about the waiting. I hated it. If I were to be thrown to a pack of wild men, or to die, I just wanted to know. I wanted it to be over with.

I had seen the stars my first day here. I would never forget that. But I still had one wish unfulfilled, and if I were to die it would be my biggest regret.

As I watched Nile and Dusk together, I wished for a love like that for myself. I'd never been in love, not in the way those two were, and I had always envied it. I'd loved my partners, my grooms, my owner, but I had never known the added spark I could see between those two. The way they curled together in sleep. The way they longed with their eyes for each other, more than affection for a partner, more than appreciation of a beautiful body or an act. They were enraptured, caught up in each other, never wanting to be apart. That is a magic I had never known.

My biggest regret.

It seemed I would die before I ever found out what that feeling was like.

Chapter Four

The cargo bay went dark. The starship rocked as if a sudden storm swept its path. No portholes decorated the bay and so we could not see what was happening. We were thrown from our mattresses. What few belongings we had were scattered across the deck. On our hands and knees, we tried to feel our way back to our beds and each other.

I found my mattress and clung to it as the ship lurched again.

Amid groans and exclamations, I heard someone crying. It sounded like Nile. I heard Dusk tell him everything was okay. Dusk placated Nile with more lies, saying we would all be fine, that they would always be together. Nile kept crying. Nile knew the truth and no amount of denial could help him. Nothing had been okay since we'd been stolen from the only homes we'd ever known.

Others began to cry. A lot of that was going on. On Anada we'd been treated as the best of the best, pampered, spoiled, always well-groomed. We worked in safe and loving environments. We had structure, and care was taken to nurture our own pleasures and desires. We had safety, love and ecstasy.

We'd been ripped from all of that and now it appeared we were going to die.

We all felt Nile's fear. We knew we were doomed before the lights went out and the starship shuddered and moaned as if in fear for itself.

I had never been to space before. Now, at 24, I wondered if I would die out here.

I clutched at my mattress as the ship seemed to jerk. Then I felt a sensation as if we were spinning. My stomach heaved into my throat. I thought I would throw up but managed to hold back.

I should have been hearing warning klaxons, alarms. But the cargo bay remained silent. I heard nothing but the muffled cries of my companions as the ship swayed this way and that. My stomach clumped into a knot.

The mayhem seemed to last for a long time. Hours.

Then everything went still. The lights finally came back on, but at half-dimness.

We all sat with our knees drawn to our chests, naked and shivering, faces etched in fear. Nile had his head against Dusk's chest, his arms wrapped tightly around him.

There was no sound from behind the locked and sealed door to the cargo bay.

The dim light made stripes of gold along the deck beyond our mattresses. I could see dust motes swirling before me as the light gilded their edges. The air smelled of boiled noodles from our last meal this morning, and the flowery perfumes our bodies could not help but give off when we sweated.

I hated not knowing anything. I hated waiting. We had been in this hold for a week. It seemed like a year.

I wanted real food. A real shower.

I tried to remember what it felt like to be outside, what sunlight looked like, how a breeze could move against my skin bringing scents of ponds and leaves from my owner's estate. I missed common sounds I had always taken for granted: crickets, birds, wind chimes, dogs barking, shuttle engines.

Whatever had happened to the ship, it was done. Perhaps we were a derelict hulk in space now, with us trapped here in its hold forever until we ran out of food and our bodies slowly died and desiccated in this forever tomb.

A sharp slice of new fear tore through my chest. We would die here, horribly and in pain. I was suddenly convinced.

22

I rested my forehead against my bent knees. Shut my eyes. My body would not stop trembling.

A loud bang jerked me from my grieving reverie.

Another bang followed, echoing throughout the hold.

We all lifted our heads and stared silently at the door.

Suddenly there was a lot of racket, like some kind of weird machine, and the door quivered outward, then went back to normal. A bit of silence was followed by more pounding. More racket.

Some of the slaves got up and went to the far end of the hold where the food was kept, standing there hugging each other. I stayed where I was, arms still wrapped around my knees and watched as the door quivered, then seemed to bend. All at once it made a great moaning sound and slowly opened, stopping halfway, the metal ragged and buckled around the edges.

I heard both masculine and feminine shouts and what sounded like a "hurrah." Then I heard the edge of a sentence, someone saying, "…so heavily locked, maybe they've hidden their treasure in here!"

The light behind the half-open door was misty and golden. I saw a black silhouette of a human, then another, and several men stepped over the threshold.

I heard their voices of shock before I could see their faces.

I gripped my legs harder and did not move. My companions hugged themselves or each other tighter.

Someone said, "What the fuck!" Someone else said, "They're people. Naked people in the cargo hold." Another voice: "Are they prisoners?" "This ain't no brig." Another: "What are they doing here? There must be at least two dozen of them."

Behind the small silhouetted group, a taller form appeared in the doorway. He towered over the rest of them and his outline showed slicked hair tied back in a short tail, a jacket that fell in a pleated skirt to his knees, and boots with some kind of ribbing that hugged his calves.

The group parted automatically for him. He strode forward and when the yellow striped lights in our hold revealed his face, I saw smooth but strong features, thick black eyebrows narrowed over dark eyes, and a generous mouth that conveyed both a scowl and a smile at the same time. His hair was jet black and the yellow lights sparked it with gold. Something glinted on his ear lobe, diamond perhaps, and on his hand. I squinted to see him clearer. Just behind the cuff of his loose sleeve a heavy, dark silver chain wrapped his wrist three times, made an arc over the top of his hand and wove through his middle three fingers.

Such jewelry on my world was called a slave bracelet.

He stood, blinking in the dimness, and his voice rang out, "Well, I'll be damned."

I watched as his dark eyes surveyed the scene, quickly taking in every detail. When his gaze landed on me and stayed—maybe because I was now the only one still sitting-- a shiver rippled down my spine.

"You," he said, pointing that braceleted hand at me. "What's your name?"

"Antares." My voice came out softer than I'd intended.

"Who are you people? What are you doing here?" he demanded.

"Anadans." My voice cracked. I took a deep breath. "The starguards came to our world. They took us and put us in here."

"You're all Anadans?" He scratched at his chin as he looked over the room once again. "I've heard of that planet but I've never been. A world, they say, of heavily guarded and strictly maintained pleasure slaves. They don't even allow tourism."

"Yes. Anada is no more. At least not as it was just a short time ago." I'd found my voice. A little. My lungs weren't shaking quite so badly now. Questions. I could answer questions. As long as I told the truth, gave whatever the other wanted, it was easy. To please others. That was all we desired.

"Stand up," he commanded.

I rose gracefully. Stood tall. Though not quite as tall as he. This man in the coat was easily the tallest human in the room. For the first time since I was 18, I had a strange impulse to clasp my hands in front of me, cover myself. I was so used to nudity I never gave it a second thought. But here and now I could not help the unease of my vulnerability.

I curled my hands to fists at my sides and held them there. The belt around my waist, which I no longer felt, became a sudden weight, its accoutrements emphasizing my lower assets which were, in this moment, cringing. Was I embarrassed? Ashamed? Why? These gruff people in leathers and fancy gun slings were nothing to me.

Except for the fact that they were everything. I did not know if they were fate or salvation. But either way, their destinies and ours were locked. For now. The starguards, it seemed, were gone. What had they done to them?

My chest moved up and down with my breaths, gleaming in perspiration from my nerves.

The stranger, undoubtedly the leader of the pack, looked me up and down. I watched his face for any reaction but saw only a slight change of moisture in his eyes and the ever-present scowl that edged up as if in humor.

"Antares is your name, you say?" the man asked me.

"Yes." I almost said 'sir' but stopped myself. He wasn't my owner. I did not owe him any respect.

"A gilded pleasure slave of Anada?"

"Yes."

"All of you? How many?"

"Thirty."

Now he turned to his crew. "My friends, this is our treasure indeed. These people are worth a fortune to us. Each one would be worth more on the black market than an average working stiff could make in ten years."

A lot of hisses and nods and general back-slapping followed from Slate's crew.

He continued, "The starship itself will fetch a good price. But these people combined are worth a hell of a lot more."

Voices broke out. "I've heard of Anada but there's so much secrecy. Who could know what was true?" "Yeah, I thought that world was a myth." "I thought the stories were just titillation for those cold nights when you're stranded at the edges of space."

"Antares," the leader said. "Come here." He gestured with his chained hand.

Slowly, I approached amid a few titters. We were streamlined creatures, made to be exquisitely beautiful. And I felt beautiful, always, never ridiculous. The man in the coat seemed to sense that. Or maybe he saw it for himself. He gestured once with his hand and they all shut up.

He looked straight into my face and said to me, "I am Slate. I am the leader here. And by the intergalactic laws of derelict ships, I claim you and your people as salvage. You belong to us, now. Do you understand?"

I nodded. I wasn't about to argue that it was apparent he had made the ship a derelict. That somehow, he had attacked an Empire ship and come out the victor. I was surprised he said nothing about the fine jewelry we wore. If he was a thief, and one good enough to get away with stealing an Empire starship, he would notice that our jewels were precious gems, and very real.

"Will you do as we say and make no trouble?"

"We are trained to obey. It is our deepest heartfelt desire. We are a peaceful kind."

Now he showed me an actual smile. "Good, then. We have an understanding."

He reached forward and grabbed my fist. I tried to jump back but he took a step forward and forced my fingers to unfold and shake his hand. This was a gesture I knew about,

26

but not used much on my planet. A gentleman's contract, some called it. But there were no gentlemen here, not among his people, nor among mine. Not to mention the fact that the contract was unfair, for he and his people, as salvage owners, would have all the say in the matter of our futures. As it had been with the starguards, we would have no voice of our own.

Chapter Five

Slate began bellowing orders to his crew. "Find them some clothes."

"We don't wear clothes," I said.

"I won't have you all distracting my crew."

"But that's what we do. What we're trained to do so that it is our very nature. There is no wrong in that."

Laughter from his people.

No sound from mine.

"Ah. I see." He scratched at the back of his head underneath his ponytail. "But if my crew is all off fucking around, when will we get any work done?"

"We can work as well. We're used to light tasks, housekeeping, general maintenance, hydroponics. Cooking."

"Cooking?" His thick eyebrows rose. "That is almost more tempting than your other, ah, gifts."

"Then you will allow us to move out of this hold?" I asked.

"There are plenty of empty staterooms for the time being, yes. But let me say this. I don't know that I can trust you yet."

"We don't know anything about fighting. Or rebellion. We are peaceful. Chosen for submission. But we must have better conditions than this until you decide what to do with us."

"But there are thirty of you."

"How many in your crew?"

He looked almost embarrassed at the question. "Twenty-one."

"More than enough of us to go around for your crew. Or if you don't like that idea, that we can be cooks and servants for each one of you, you can lock us in our staterooms. At least we would have some human comforts there. Like showers and decent food."

He pondered that for a moment, looking intently into my eyes. "You say you know nothing of rebellion or fighting, but you certainly are a demanding little pleasure slave, now, aren't you?"

I did not blink. "We've been cooped up here for far too long," I replied calmly.

He crossed his arms over his big chest. His eyes narrowed. "You will make no demands from me. And you will have to earn your trust."

"I swear to you, we will do anything for you and your crew. It's how we're made."

"I'm sure it is."

"Please. Please don't leave us locked in down here."

"I never intended it. You will have your staterooms. There are more than enough. But you will be locked within them, at least for the time being. We intend to dispose of this starship as soon as possible. After that, other arrangements will have to be made. My own ship is far too small for the lot of you."

"Thank you." The words rushed from me. I knew I must have looked desperate, but I was also so relieved. Though we survived, we were suffering in this hold. Slowly dying.

This man. He seemed to be somewhat of a tyrant, as well as a rogue and a thief. But somewhere in his gaze I saw a heart, something I hadn't seen since Anada had been invaded. And though the starguards were themselves human, they were bound by strict Empire law. 'Heart' in the Empire was seen as weakness.

But Slate did not operate under Empire law. He was a much freer man and his stature and demeanor reflected this.

He did not reply to my thanks but merely turned away from me and exited the hold, giving orders to his people as he went. His last order repeated one of his initial demands. "Get these people some clothes."

He had to know we wouldn't wear them. But that was the least of our concerns. Soon we would be out of here and given hot showers or baths. We would have real food we could cook for ourselves, and beds for sleeping and other things. This was better than anything the starguards could ever think to give us.

I knew Slate would have to acquiesce on a few things I had suggested, for now he oversaw 51 people instead of 21, and attention would have to be given to meals, cleaning up after meals, doing laundry, making beds. With slaves at the ready, he would not be able to resist our help.

And pleasure for free for the asking? With the most highly trained, pampered and powdered pleasure slaves in the known galaxy? I made a mental bet most of his crew wouldn't last the night, the women as well as the men, before asking many of us for special favors.

*

For space pirates, Slate and his crew were pretty well organized.

One of his crewmen, Tahir, made a list of all our names and assigned us to staterooms. If any of us wanted to share, he allowed it, which was good for Nile and Dusk who could never bear to be apart.

More crewmembers rounded up clothing. It consisted of uniform style pants and pullover shirts, all black. The sort of undergarments starguards wore beneath their armor.

After years of being nude, the idea of clothing was disgusting to us. Clothing chafes when you're not used it. It feels like a cage. A few of us sniffed at the pile of garments offered, but there were no takers.

Tahir laughed and said to his cohort, "Slate's gonna be pissed. These people are spoiled. I think they'll be wanting fine silks or nothing else."

None of Slate's crew touched us as they were rounding us up and getting us settled, but their eyes told us they wanted to. We were trained to elicit stares. That was what we loved. We preened from that kind of attention. We were sculpted beauties, after all.

Already some of us had picked their marks, standing closer to one crewmember over another, following him or her about the room. The crew were rogues and thieves. They wore leather and braids, guns and thigh boots. They had less morals than the starguards, but they were clearly devoted to Slate. His orders not to touch us stood. For now. But I observed the flush on the cheeks of some of them, the heightened awareness of us, the tense body language, the tart/sweet perspiration of arousal. Their eyes were bright. And they watched us hungrily.

Ocean and Amethyst decided to share a stateroom. They invited me to join them. "Keep the family together," they said. But I declined. I loved them, but three to a room unnerved me right now. I needed time alone. I was going through all sorts of changes since the invasion, thoughts I'd never had before, impatience and bitterness winning over my usual complacency. I had been so happy for so long. All that had been taken from me. We were all going through that, but everyone reacted differently. Amethyst became more sexually extroverted. Nile cried often in Dusk's arms. Ocean coupled with anyone who would have him. I went silent.

I wanted time off. Time alone.

A man with a fedora hat decorated with a short, purple feather brought me to my stateroom. I said nothing to him. As he closed the door, I did not even thank him.

The staterooms were as plain as the rec room Amethyst and I had been taken to that first day with the three starguards. The bulkheads, an ugly off-white, seemed to suck

31

energy from the room. On the bed draped a gray cover with a rough texture I immediately hated. The lighting, still at half-power, had an uncomfortable foggy glow.

But on one side of the room, a miracle. An oval porthole stretched horizontally at eye-level. And beyond the clear window swam endless fields of stars. I went to it and leaned my forehead against the glass. It was cool and smooth. For a long time I stared at distant flickering suns like spilled crystals upon the shadow of time. Something inside my chest shifted in a kind of hollow ache. What were their names, I wondered. And where did they think they were going?

The room came with its own bath and I immediately began to fill the tub while reading the instructions about the recycled water system, and how the tub would only fill to a certain level before automatically shutting off.

Slowly I removed my belt, noting the creases it had made into the skin at my hips and groin. I unfastened the leather from between my legs and unclasped the ring around my genitalia. I left the rest of my jewelry on. Water wouldn't hurt it and it would clean the jewels of my rings, making them shinier.

If there was such a thing as paradise away from Anada, it was a tub of hot water and the silence of steam rising around me as I sank into it. I submerged myself as far as I could under the water, letting my hair snake around my shoulders, closing my eyes as the liquid muted my hearing and covered my face.

I held my breath for a long time, then came up to rub my gleaming chest and legs with a liquid soap that came out of the wall at the touch of a button.

I soaped up my entire body in what became a transcendent experience. I was surprised to find myself physically un-aroused when everything felt so good. Maybe I was just that tired. It was so relaxing, this bath I'd waited so long for, that my body went limp all over. As if it were already asleep in some faraway dream where reality, war, starguards and space thieves had no meaning or form. They were shadows on a horizon too distant to see.

I soaped my hair twice. Under the water, I combed it out with my fingers. I sat up again and braided it so it hung down the left side of my shoulder.

I thoroughly cleaned the rest of my body, taking time with a soft cloth over my genitals and in-between my buttocks. My libido still remained dormant. I had no sensation, not even a tingle of arousal though the bath itself was pure pleasure. Despite the exhilaration of cleanliness, I was wrung out, overly tired.

I rose lazily, swaying, the water cascading off my shining skin. There was a warm dryer off to my right and I stood under it letting the currents brush over and around me.

The utopia of the bed, despite its horrible gray colored covers, beckoned. I fell naked into it, pulling the pillow to my chest, and slept.

Chapter Six

I wish I could remember all of my dreams. But usually I remember only the ones just before waking.

That first night in my stateroom, all alone, I dreamed of Anada, something I hadn't done since being taken away from my home. I dreamed I was back in my training harem.

There, we had lived and trained in vast arboretums with skylights that opened to the sun and stars. In the greenhouse environment, plants grew and thrived. So did humans.

We had sparkling pools and frothing fountains with water clear as blue topaz to play in. Mosaic tile decorated the pool bottoms and the decks where plush pillows and beds of rising red and silver silks, curtained or open to the sunlight, enclosed us in their cool softness. Amid writhing bouts of ecstasy we also got tons of exercise. Our bodies became trim and toned.

We drank juices that increased our libidos. Grooms attended to our depilatory process which took months and resulted in permanent hairlessness below our necks. Our skin was bathed daily in softening agents until we glowed.

Our teachings included the philosophies of pleasure as well as physical, until all mental shame vanished. Though Anada was an openly bisexual culture where pleasure was considered a natural focus, this did not mean we were immune to little poisons that could stain the heart. Peer pressure and childish criticism still occurred. Even the most beautiful and endowed of us had insecurities from youth that needed to be wiped away.

In my dream, memory took me back to a day with one of my trainees, a dark-eyed boy named Lake. He was one of my favorites, an Adonis with glossy black hair and a natural radiance to him. He stood a few inches shorter than me, with a compact, naturally tanned body and one of the most beautiful cocks I'd ever seen. It was average in size, but lovely as a rare flower. It was one of those that never turned red even in the heights of ecstasy. The shaft was golden and the glans was the color of pale pink soap bubbles. People liked to say boys with that coloring ran cool, not hot, but really it was simple genetics. In truth, he ran hotter than most.

Today Lake sat in the shallows of the triangle pool while a group of nymphs, all full-breasted and shining, lounged on the pool edge and kept glancing at him and whispering among themselves. Occasionally they kissed and licked each other, exposing themselves sweetly, obviously trying to get his attention. But he never even looked up.

Someone had told me they'd seen him earlier alone by the napping alcoves, trying to hide the fact that he was crying.

As one of my charges, it was my duty to oversee not only his sexual training, but his mental well-being, too.

I came down the shallow steps and sat down next to him. "Lake." Only when I said his name did he seem to come to awareness.

"Antares. Hi." He leaned back on the top step, revealing his cock bobbing under the water.

Training Lake was a treat because he was always so eager. Such a sweet boy, he couldn't always hold back and I got a lot of unexpected face-fulls of his exuberant orgasms before I could even take him fully in my mouth. He could come from one stroke of my hand. The trick was to teach him to hold off a little, relax. He ran so hot he could derive pleasure from orgasm only. Foreplay became after-play for him if he didn't fall right to sleep. I was still working on the right way for him to be lovingly distracted without outright punishing his balls or the head of his cock so he could ride the journey up at a slower pace and enjoy himself in sex, not to mention pleasuring a partner. And pleasuring others without taking away from self-enjoyment was the ultimate priority of good training.

I put my arms around him. "Why are you sad today?"

"I'm failing at this, aren't I? Tell me the truth." His mouth turned down. His eyes filled.

I hugged him tighter, kissed the slick hair at his temple. His eyes were so dark and languid I wanted to kiss them, too, lick the tears, push him back and fill him up.

He smelled of chlorine and fresh air. I knew his flavor well. Apple. Brown sugar. He was a deep wind hiding in the leaves, always ready to explode. I liked that about him. He would be fine. He just had to be patient.

"Come with me," I said, moving up from the water, tugging at his arm.

He floated forward and stood, walking with me up the steps. We dried each other off. I took the towel and slowly wiped it across his back, his shoulders, then his chest. I knelt before him and folded the towel around one leg, then the other. His thighs were strong and taut. I blotted at them. His cock jerked up and swayed in front of my face.

"Oh," he said so sweet, biting down on his lip. "Please just lick it a little."

"No." I avoided it altogether, not even a brush of his balls.

He jutted his hips forward. I ignored the gesture and stood, taking his hand. "Come over here."

He followed eagerly and when I approached the red bed with the wispy, see-through curtains that were the colors of storm clouds, he jumped up on the red cover and lay back so willing, his hair, still damp on the ends, spread out around his head.

After closing the curtains for semi-privacy—though anyone could see us if they wanted—I knelt on the bed beside him. He raised his hands up like a baby waiting to be picked up.

I shook my head. "Lake, you're going to pleasure me."

"I will but I can't hold on. Please, Antares, do me first!" He often promised this, but then he would fall asleep with his essence still glistening on his cock, and forget all about promises until he woke hard again and the cycle continued.

"You were just crying to me that you thought you were failing. Let's prove it together that you're not."

He lowered his arms. His brow wrinkled as he sat up, knees bending. "I know I'm terrible. I spill too soon. I'm hopeless."

"You're not hopeless." I lay back on the cushions and grasped his wrist. "Touch me here for now." I placed his hand against my chest. "And kiss me, you little imp. And do not let that cock touch any part of my body as you do this."

"But then how can I hold you and touch you if I can't press against you?"

I frowned at him. "Figure it out. But if you touch me with that thing I swear to you I'll lock you in the dorm for a whole day alone. No one to touch or to touch you for a full day and a night!"

He pressed his lips tight in a grimace, but nodded. "Okay. Please don't be mad at me." His eyes blinked at more tears. He knew his charms, he just worked them wrong. Right now he was trying to get me to take him in my arms, soothe and comfort him.

"Sweetheart, I could never be mad at you. This is work now. You just need to learn to do the job."

The tears brimmed over and dotted his cheeks. How I wanted to wipe them away with my fingers, my lips. Instead, I reached out and smacked him on the ass. Not hard. Just enough to get his attention.

"Did you hear what I asked you to do? I'm waiting."

He sniffed, gulped. His damp lashes glittered. "You said not to touch you, um, um. You said, you said to, to kiss you."

"That's right, baby. You know what to do." I waited. His hand was a fist at my chest. He took a few deep breaths. If he began to sob I wasn't sure what I would do then.

Finally, licking his pretty pink lips, he moved so that his knees were bent and he could lean over me without his lower body coming into contact with mine. He flattened his palm against my chest, put his other hand beside my head to support his weight, and leaned down.

The kiss was not skillful. But it was delightfully innocent, better than if he'd been trying too hard. His lips touched mine with a warm pressure. He did not immediately open his mouth. If he was holding back to punish me, I would be disappointed. I preferred to think he was building himself up, doling out his gift as I'd tried to teach him before, taking his time.

I lounged, pliant and unmoving, and waited for further developments, leaving all decision to him. If he made the wrong one, I'd gently guide him. There was no shame here in the harem. We did not teach by that method. But neither did we allow little brats like him to take advantage of the gentleness and encouragement. If he needed sternness, he would get it. And right now I was determined he would not come until I told him to. If I had to pinch the tip of his cock to keep him from coming, I would. I made the mistake once days ago of flicking it with my finger, hoping to startle him from his over-arousal, and he ended up orgasming anyway.

Now his kiss pressed at my lips, still closed, but moving to one corner of my mouth, then the other, dry but smooth, shy but not chaste. His hand was hot against my chest, heavy but not pushing.

I waited, letting him do what he wanted.

He seemed unsure but I could be very patient. I was not turned off by difficult men. Quite the contrary.

38

At last his tongue darted out, licking at the opening between my lips. Lightly. Delicately. The edge of dampness wetting me but never sloppy. Slowly, I opened my mouth. Nothing more. His tongue probed hesitantly. Taste of salt and wind. What a gem he could be when he put his mind to it.

His hand began to move against my chest. Lightly at first, skimming with his fingertips and the fleshy parts of his palm. My skin reacted. My nipples hardened at just that simple motion.

His palm encountered one and he felt the erect bud, ran his fingers over it, around it, then took it between his thumb and forefinger as he continued to invade my mouth.

I stretched in pleasure and could no longer keep my tongue still. It encountered his, pressed, coming together with his in my mouth, licking, pressing, twining.

When he came up for air, his cheeks had a bit of pink in them I'd never seen before. In the past, there'd never been time with him for the flush and blush. I smiled at him. "Keep going. It's great."

He kneaded my other nipple now, then bent and took it into his mouth, gently licking first before finally sucking it until it stood straight up, a tiny puckered bud of skin.

He came up and leaned over me, looking down into my eyes. "I can't take it. Antares, I think I'm going to die. I'm going to burst."

"No, you won't. Don't stop now. Take your mind away from yourself. Think of the other person, what you're doing to them."

He groaned. "It hurts," he whined.

I squeezed his hand at my chest. Watched him wince. "No it doesn't. Arousal feels good, amazing. Absorb it into yourself and carry on. You'll get there. You just don't have to rush."

He whined a little more. I did not chastise him. I merely waited. When he became bored with the fact that his whining was getting him nowhere, he turned his attention back to me.

He kissed me again with full tongue this time. He lowered his head and nuzzled my neck, nipping at the skin. Over his shoulder I could see his ass in the air as he held himself aloft, away from me and the bed and any friction that might make him come. I wanted to run my hands all over that ass. Soon enough.

He licked his way down my chest. The air cooled each damp stripe he made across my pecks, my ribs. My cock swayed. So ripe for him. But I was not desperate. I'd already come twice earlier that morning, once inside the fiery catacombs of Amethyst when I woke in my bed with her curled beside me. A second time in some nameless blond kid's relentlessly sucking mouth at the hot tub.

Further Lake went, down to my belly button. He played with it, darting his tongue inside, tickling a little. My stomach muscles quivered.

He licked my hips, but not my cock. That he nuzzled, as if he knew not to go too fast or I'd surely correct him.

For awhile he lapped at the inside of both my thighs before working his way to my feet and bathing each toe in delicious suckling. I could see him, his cock jutting hard between his legs, bouncing up and down, begging to be touched. It was lovely and I watched as drop after drop of clear fluid oozed from the tip.

Finally he came back up to center himself, gazing at my erection with parted lips. He did not complain anymore about his own burgeoning state. I would commend him for that later.

"Balls first," I said gently.

He pushed my cock back against my belly, his hand softly encircled about it, and licked at the loose skin of my balls. He didn't stop until they were completely wet. Then he carefully sucked one ball into his mouth, tonguing it, then the other. I felt them tighten at the attention. My cock throbbed but I was not close. Not yet.

With quick little licks, Lake worked his way up my shaft. "Do not put it into your mouth until it is gleaming," I instructed.

He obeyed, tonguing it all over and up and down. Finally he took the tip into his mouth, his big eyes looking at me for approval.

I nodded and he began to suck.

"Work your tongue," I told him.

I felt it wriggling against the underside of my cock.

"Wonderful," I said. "Now go down a little more."

The classes in deep-throating were for second-years only. He easily took me in half-way, and with enthusiasm. Was he only looking to hurry toward his own pleasure? Or did he really want to succeed?

"You're doing good," I said. "How's that cock of yours?"

He came up off me, licking the tip twice before answering. "I wanna come so bad." He straightened up on his knees, showing me how hard and ready he was. Trying not to be too proud, but failing.

I smiled at him. "Good."

"I need it." His voice shivered. He made a gesture as if to touch himself.

"Don't!"

He pouted.

"Soon."

He sighed, bent over and went back to work on me.

I raised myself up on my elbows. "Is it good and wet?" I asked.

He licked up and I popped out of his mouth. He looked pleased at his accomplishment. "Yes."

"Good because I'm going to fuck you now."

His head bowed. "Now?"

"Yep."

"But I --"

"I know. You haven't done it before. This is your lesson today, too."

"Nile tried to once. It hurt and he stopped. I don't think I'm ready."

"Nile?" I sat all the way up. "You know you're only supposed to do that with your trainers. Especially if you're a virgin!"

"I know." Sheepish, he hung his head. "I only told you because I'm not ready, Antares. I'm not!" More whining. And I thought we'd gotten over that.

I said, "You need a skilled trainer. You know that!"

More pouting. More tears now, filling up his depthless eyes. "I need to come first," he protested, chin on his chest.

"No. You don't. Stop crying right now and look at me."

He looked up, sniffling again. Babies. What to do with them.

"Look, if you come first it won't be as pleasurable. Besides, you'll fall asleep on me and the lesson will be a waste. Do you understand?"

He grudgingly nodded. His cock bobbed as if in agreement, the pretty pink tip still dripping.

In the alcove above the bed were plenty of elixirs. I chose a rose-colored bottle. "Turn around," I ordered.

He obeyed. His perfect backside faced me now, tan and firm.

"Head down, ass up," I told him.

Without giving any attention to his cock and balls, I slowly oiled him between his buttocks. His reaction to getting any physical attention at all was to spread his legs and stick his butt up higher. So I praised him.

I rubbed the oil over his puckered opening and teased it. He opened to my finger without comment but also without tension. "You're doing so good, Lake. Does it hurt?"

He shook his head, then mumbled something.

"What?"

"Your cock is way bigger than that."

"You'll be fine. We'll take it slow."

He mumbled something else, but I did not ask him to repeat it.

I moved my finger in and out slowly, letting him get used to it. A little more oil and patience, and another finger went in beside it. Then a third. "Okay?" I asked.

"Fuck. Damn. Yes!"

That made me grin. "Then you're ready, I think."

He said nothing.

I removed my fingers and positioned my cock. He stayed quite still and I wanted to reward him for that. "You're doing great, sweetheart. I'm going to fuck you now, but real slow at first. If it hurts, you tell me." And then I pushed. To offset any shock for him, I finally gave him what he'd been wanting all along. I reached around his waist and took his cock in my hand. As I entered him, I gave him a long, smooth stroke.

"Oh!" He caught his breath. Again, "Oh!"

Before he knew it, I had fully impaled him.

"More," he said softly.

I stroked him again. He didn't spill. I praised him over and over and then began to thrust.

"You're doing it now," I said.

"Oh, it's so good. So good!" At that I had him rocking back on me, pulling forward, rocking back again, and I don't even think he knew how good it was for me now. He was in his own world of ecstasy, and it was holding, holding. I knew he'd never experienced anything like it.

He made more excited noises. With one hand I stroked his cock. My other hand cupped and fondled the smooth cheeks of his ass.

I made sure I was angled just right, hitting that sweet spot inside him over and over. It rendered him incoherent, poised on the brink of something life-changing.

His ass so neat and firm. The way it gripped me, tight and hot. The way he bore back on me as if he could not get enough.

I saw the sunlight through the cloudy curtains catch the fibers and twinkle. The fragrance of the splashing fountains, the hot tiles, the cool grasses washed over us. The sheets of the bed were red and the mattress soft against us. A coolness spread over me like a little trapped breeze, then my skin blazed forth. I cried out. Lake cried out. I pushed deep into him, pressed my chest against his back and felt his cock spasm in my hand as I emptied myself inside him.

Lake was one of those boys with an abundance of milk. It sprayed the sheets and bed, but he didn't care. He collapsed in his own dampness and turned as I pulled gently out so he could face me.

"Antares, that was the best ever." He put his arms around my shoulders and I reached out to comb back his silken hair.

"You're not a failure. You just need practice. Like that. Every day," I said.

I kissed his forehead. He tilted his head up, begging for a kiss on his lips. I complied against his summery, sleepy smile. His hands caressed my back and sides.

"I love you, Antares." He yawned.

I caressed his cheek and under his chin as his eyes slowly closed. He was asleep in seconds.

I extricated myself from his arms and pushed the curtain open. He slept like baby on his side, arms up to his chest and knees bent.

I got up leaving the curtain parted so people could see the bed was occupied, and went for a swim. Everywhere naked bodies cavorted, glimmered, clashed in the light. Swollen sexual organs was the norm. I smiled. How I loved this place where I could forget who I was, where all my needs were met, where my world was serene and safe and full of ecstasy.

44

Soon I forgot the pang I felt when Lake told me he loved me.

Soon I was swimming and love was everywhere, a surrounding liquid of bliss, brilliant, sleek, flower-scented. A delicacy of inner seas, a realm of ageless longing met again and again.

Chapter Seven

I woke slowly from the dream, still seeing the cool blue pool around me, feeling the liquid of it against my skin. I stretched my legs out, forgetting for a moment where I was. The dream was so real. I thought I could taste chlorinated water on my lips. I looked down. Normally such a dream would arouse me, but I was soft, still at peace, my body slow to wake.

I opened my eyes and everything was wrong, different. No sunshine. No grass-scented breezes.

I heard a rapid pounding. I re-oriented myself slowly as everything came into focus. The stateroom. The rough gray bed. The soft hum of starship technology running through the bulkheads.

The pounding continued, along with a door buzzer sound, and I realized someone was at the door.

I got up, the deck slick and cool against my feet. How long had I slept?

I went to the door and pushed the unlock button so it would open.

A man I did not know wearing a green tank top and black leather trousers said, "We locked you in. Weren't you told not to use the inside lock?"

I shook my head.

"Slate wants to see you." He looked me up and down. He had no hair on his head, which highlighted the tattoo of fighting dragons that wrapped about his skull. It was a fine piece of art with vivid reds, greens and purples. Their tails wrapped about his ears.

"And put some clothes on," he added.

"Why does Slate want to see me?"

"I don't know. He has questions, I guess. You're the one who answered them before when no one else would speak up. I guess he figures you're talkative."

"Can I pee first?"

He shrugged like he didn't care, then said, "Don't you have clothes?"

"No."

"A robe? Anything?"

"I have an emerald-studded belt."

His face contorted into an impatient grimace.

I went into the bathroom and finished quickly, then grabbed my leather belt and put it on. Instantly I felt more at home. The belt was a part of me.

When I came to the door again the man said, "The staterooms come with robes. Just take one."

I stood unmoving.

"Please?" He exhaled loudly in frustration.

I went to the bathroom closet and found a white cover up complete with belt. I draped it over my shoulders. Nothing more. I walked back to the door and asked, "Will this do?"

"Yeah. Can you put it on?"

To placate him, I pushed my arms through the soft sleeves. It wasn't as uncomfortable as I expected, but it still felt all wrong. I refused to fasten the belt. The robe hung open in front. I pulled my braid free of the collar. The white cloth fell to my thighs, the hem just above my knees.

The man rolled his eyes and said, "Follow me."

Slate had taken over the captain's quarters. There were tablets and lightboards everywhere. Metal boxes sat three-high in two corners. The bed in the sleeping alcove was rumpled and clothes and belts littered the deck.

Slate wore a white cotton pullover and a black leather vest. His skirted coat was draped over the back of his chair. He had on black jeans but no fancy boots this time. His feet were bare. He still had the slave-chain on his wrist and fingers, dark silver links that wrapped over his hand and around his wrist three times. I wondered if it meant something, or if he just liked the fashion.

His black hair was down, wispy about the ears and the collar of his shirt. The look he gave me as I entered his rooms was tired but hard. I watched as his eyes traveled down the length of my body. He couldn't help himself, of course. We pleasure slaves were primed to draw the eye.

Slate sat behind a curving counter that was covered with devices. Some looked broken, showing their wires. Behind him I saw an oval porthole like the one in my own stateroom, the stars sliding by. A pang of longing rose from my stomach.

"Antares." Slate got up from the desk and approached me, arm outstretched. The gentleman's handshake. I remembered he liked it.

This time I reached back. Our hands met for the second time in two days. His grip was warm and strong, the skin of his palms smooth, un-callused. He had never been a menial laborer, then, but were those tiny scars on his upper hands? I couldn't be sure, but definite markings marred the flesh. Maybe it was only a change in his natural skin pigment.

Slate stepped back and gestured to my robe. "It's meant to be fastened in the front."

"It makes me feel like I can't breathe," I quickly replied.

He acted as if he didn't hear me, and moved past me, dismissing the man who'd brought me to his door and hitting the close button.

He came back into the room and approached his desk. His back to me, he said, "Take a seat if you'd like."

A chair with the same gray and scratchy texture as my bedcover stood in front of the desk. I moved over to it and sat.

"I'm sorry if my nudity bothers you."

He took his own seat and looked at me. "No, you're not."

My mouth opened to reply but nothing came out.

"Look, I understand that everything in your life has changed, that you're a victim of war and all that. But that's the way of the universe. It's shit and that's reality. But out here in space, well, the rest of us aren't used to just walking around in the altogether. Change happens. People adapt."

"Why should I care about new rules or customs? Nothing changes. Not for us. I had a family unit, security. Now I have nothing."

"Well, I can't fix that."

"Why would you? We're commodities. You said it yourself in the hold. You can sell us for more combined than this Empire starship is worth."

His dark eyes flashed. "Yes. And that's why I brought you here."

I smiled, but for once I didn't feel it. "To test the merchandise maybe?"

He did not respond to that. Instead he said, "To have a discussion with you. I'm not in the business of dealing in human cargo."

"Well, I don't see what I can do to help you with that. Besides, I thought I heard you promise fortunes to your crew from us."

"What I mean is, I may be a thief. I may not care about galactic law. But I have some places where I draw the line. I've discussed this with my crew. They all understand. I'm uncomfortable with human cargo."

"Well what are you going to do, then? You technically own us now."

He shook his head. I saw distrust in his gaze, and indecision. "Can your people even take care of themselves if I set you down on an alien world somewhere in a big city where you could disappear?"

Stunned at the question, for a moment I couldn't think. I'd never fathomed being on my own before. Never even fantasized about it. It was why I'd consented to pleasure slavery. With consent came an arena where all decisions were taken and made for me. It might sound strange, but it was a freeing sensation. I didn't have to think. I simply responded. It might sound odd to state this, but it was completely freeing for me.

I watched him for a moment as he waited patiently for my answer. The starlight shone through his hair from the oval window behind him. His head glimmered.

"I chose my life. I worked hard for it," I began. "I wanted a protected life where I didn't have to make decisions. Where I didn't have to think beyond pleasure and my gifts and talents for it. Maybe I'm spoiled, but I worked for it. My position came with training, devotion, a commitment to perfection. I put everything into this life. What would I do in some alien city?"

His face was still, contemplative. "Like I said. Life's shit. You adapt. How old are you?"

"24."

"You're still young. You seem to have a mind. Can you read? Can you write?"

I nodded. "Of course."

"What about the others?"

"We're all schooled."

"But could they survive?"

"Are you saying you're willing to free us?"

"I'm saying I'm considering it."

"And what we're worth—you'd lose all that."

He offered a rather condescending smile. "I have money. I'm a very good thief."

All the right words were being said, a best possible outcome considering all we had lost and the doomed fates we'd faced with the starguards. So why did my stomach quiver, my chest constrict? Why this feeling of panic?

I clasped my hands in front of me to quell their shaking. I looked down. "I don't know," I said.

"You don't know what?"

I looked at him through my eyelashes. "I don't know if we can survive." As I spoke those words I saw Lake's sad, sweet face. Heard him say, *I'm failing at this, aren't I? I'm terrible. I'm hopeless.* Was I giving up on myself, my people, without even thinking of trying? Was I just a jeweled brat in a pretty body?

But no. I lived for sensuality. It was my art. Such a natural thing. Why should my art be seen as anything less than a singer, a writer, an actor—a thief? I had been a success in my life, even if only for a few years.

I looked straight into the pirate's eyes. "What if you were caught, captured? Taken away to prison? What if everything you now have just vanished? And you couldn't do any of it anymore? Would you like it? Would you like it if someone asked you, if not by force, then to voluntarily change your nature?"

His chest rose with his breath. His shoulders straightened. He put his hand to the bridge of his nose and rubbed as if too tired to even be having this conversation. Finally he said, "What makes you think I haven't?"

We stared at each other.

Finally, he said, "No. I would not like it."

I realized tears had risen to my eyes. I blinked. I had not cried since the invasion. "Then let's figure out another way."

My hands in my lap were sweating. A strange heat began to break out all over my skin. The stars behind Slate's head spun a little. "Are we moving fast?" I asked.

"On autopilot in slide-space where we can't be traced. Why?"

"I can feel it."

"You shouldn't be able to feel it at all."

But I was so hot, and more pangs stabbed at my stomach. "Antares?"

I saw him stand and the movement made me suddenly dizzy.

"Are you ill?"

I tried to shake my head, clear the fog. "I'm fine."

"When was the last time you ate?"

"I don't remember."

I saw him move closer, smelled the leather of his vest.

My mind was whirling. All I could think about was that we were about to be abandoned, all 30 of us from the hold, and that our fates on the streets of some alien city might be worse than if we were outright sold to rich bidders. At least with a wealthy owner, there might be a chance for decent treatment, nice homes. The underbelly of the galaxy held few promises, but the streets of a big city seemed even more foreboding.

I looked up when I felt something prod my arm. "Here."

Slate stood next to me, waving a nutri-bar in my face. In his other hand he had a glass of water.

My hands were shaking when I took them from him. He did not comment. For a moment he just watched me as I bit into the bar. Immediately my mouth watered. I nearly swallowed the first bite whole. After the second bite, that fast, my head began to clear.

I'd been stupid not to take care of myself, extenuating circumstances or not.

Slate made a 'humph' sound under his breath and moved back into his chair.

As if no time had elapsed, he said, "You want to figure out another way, I'm listening."

I chewed and swallowed, finally able to taste what I was eating. It was surprisingly sweet and moist, like some kind of chewy cake. "I think we'd be better off if you just sold us like you thought about doing in the first place. At least we wouldn't be homeless in a strange place."

"I don't have trusted resources for such a thing. I told you, I don't deal in live cargo."

I was thinking clearer now. My mind quickly assessed everything I knew about this man as well as what I read off him. "You can find them," I said. "What if we worked together? Us and your crew. We vet the buyers. Together. Let my people help make their own choices in the process?"

Frowning, he said, "That's what you want? Not freedom? Not to go your own way?"

"We're not equipped. You'd be abandoning us. This way, well, you'd make a lot of money and everyone would be happy."

"This is the oddest deal I have ever encountered, and believe me, I've encountered a lot. But pleasure slaves helping to sell themselves—I must be dreaming. It's insane."

"It's more sane than forcing someone to go somewhere against their will. More sane than abandoning 30 people alone and defenseless on some planet, with no money and perhaps not even speaking the language."

He shook his head. "It will take too long. I plan to liquidate this ship and move on in a matter of weeks. Selling thirty pleasure slaves on the black market while vetting each and every potential buyer could take, well, a long time."

"Not with us helping. And you can hold off on this starship sale for a little while, can't you? With the money you'll be making off us, it's a far better deal."

He looked frustrated that he couldn't argue with that. A gleam came into his eyes. "You're all a distraction to my crew. I don't—I can't—"

"Can't what? Your crew aren't angels. You can't tell me you don't put up with a little fucking around."

His eyebrows rose. "I never said that. I'm no prude."

"Then what's the problem? It's a good plan. You'll be a winner twice over, rid of us, and a much wealthier man. Bonuses for your crew. Some off-duty harmless play. Your crew will love you. They'll be more devoted than ever."

"They teach you negotiation in pleasure slave school?"

His tone annoyed me.

His glare went right through me. His attitude was pissing me off and I never lost my temper. On Anada I'd been supremely level in my moods, complacent and happy every day from my first day in the harem until just a week ago.

He had seemed so reasonable when this discussion began. Now I began to have my doubts. My stomach clamped. With a still-shaking hand, I placed my water on the edge of his desk.

I said, "Everything's negotiation. Especially on planets with generations of peace. That's how peace is kept."

His mouth turned down. His brows narrowed. He stared at me for some seconds, and then without warning let out a long, low, rumbling laugh.

He stood, leaning over his desk with a big grin, placing both hands flat on the surface amid all the mess. "I do like this plan. But shouldn't you ask the others first?"

"I don't have to. They'll want this. They've never wanted anything else. We weren't forced into this, you know. All of us chose to be who we are."

He clapped his hands together. "Okay, then. Go and get yourself a proper meal. I'll talk to my crew. I'll contact some sources, shady as they are, and we'll get things started."

I stood, still a little shaky. "Thank you."

My robe swished back. My braid slid over my shoulder and down my back. I expected him to look me up and down again, but he didn't. Instead, he turned away in dismissal, as if I'd already left the room.

The bald man with the dragon tattoos stood in the corridor waiting for me. His eyes lingered on my naked body, as expected.

I said to him, nonchalantly, "Don't look so hungry. You're going to be well-fed very very soon."

He tilted his head. "Huh?"

"I'm to get a proper meal," I answered.

"Uh, oh. I'll have a tray sent to your room. It would've been done earlier, but you'd locked your door and weren't answering."

"Sorry for that," I quipped. I moved forward. Despite a lot of twists and turns, my mind had memorized the route back to my room.

This time, I led.

Chapter Eight

After I'd eaten, I sat on my bed with my knees drawn up and stared at the bulkheads. I thought about Lake again, how convinced he'd been that he wasn't good enough for what he wanted. I wondered what had become of him.

Slate was on my mind, too. His handsomeness was a bit unnerving, but I could control myself there. Slate had Lake's lovely coloring, but they couldn't have been more different. Still, he was my type, not so young and with a bit of mileage on him.

I thought about seducing him but then dismissed it. I wanted our relationship uncomplicated. Sex didn't have to complicate things, but usually it came with drama when there were no rules, and when you had a boatload of humans who'd never met a true pleasure slave before.

I stood by the porthole and watched the stars for a time.

I searched the room, every cupboard, drawer and closet. As bare as the stateroom was, I found things: stacks of towels, new toothbrushes, razors, scents, lotions, lube, clothes, belts. In some drawers I found dust. In others strange clear cubes, a tablet, an old belt buckle with an Empire triangle design, a gold coin, a blue stylus, two unopened jars of nuts, two bottles of wine, three plastic cups.

I took the tablet and one of the bottles of wine to the bed, sat against the pillows. The gray cover chafed at my skin but I was more interested in the tablet.

It opened for me right away once I figured out how to turn it on.

There was a whole universe there.

I found music, pictures, holo-films, games, books. For awhile I read at random, whatever came up when I tapped a figure. Something about an alien sports team winning a medal. Something else about a House of Commons on a planet called Ele. An article about giant arachnids. Of course I'd seen films, read books, but Anada was isolated. We did not get outside source information for anything other than learning our place in the galaxy geographically speaking. We knew of the Empire, of course, and their war. None of it affected us.

Or so we thought. Our fates did not lie in ignorance so much as passivity. It was nice to be a peaceful planet. It was not nice to have it so easily taken from us.

Refusing to think more on it, I found a music button and spent time fiddling around until I found something I liked. Slowly, I drank the whole bottle of wine, liking that it made me care less about things. I let the music play, some wild and raucous with violent lyrics, some slower, angsting on love.

I lay back and fell asleep, remembering better times.

I woke to another tray of food brought to my door, this time by a woman with blue hair and pierces through her nose and lips. She stared at my groin. I cocked a hip and she finally looked up. "They said you were the prettiest."

"Who?"

She shrugged. "Huh, they were right."

She said nothing to me about Slate and his plan; if he'd talked to the crew yet, put things in motion, I couldn't know. It had only been a half day. I didn't ask.

The door shut and locked.

I ate and listened to more music. With renewed energy, I searched the whole place again but found nothing new.

I moved around the room restlessly, flinging my robe over my head, catching it, twisting it, tying it in knots. I played an exercise vid on the tablet and tried to follow it. I sprawled across the bed in abandon, naked, somersaulting my legs over my head. Jumping up, running to the bathroom door, turning and running back to the bed.

I was 24. I had a lot of energy. No one was making use of it.

Finally, I grabbed the second bottle of wine and watched some weird cartoon. Later, half the wine gone, I drifted into a doze. The tablet clattered to the deck. I didn't care.

I dreamed the harem again, all springtime and feathery, but nothing specific this time. It was comforting, nonetheless.

*

Mid-morning, the door opened. The blue-haired woman again. "Slate wants to meet with you," she said. She looked me up and down. "Clothed, preferably."

"I know it's preferable for him, but not for me." I didn't realize how rude I sounded until the words were out. I never spoke to others in that way before. Well, war changed people. Softer, I said, "Just a second."

I went to the bed and grabbed the white robe, undoing the knotted sleeves and putting it on. This time I crossed the front over my body and tied the belt.

"Better?" I asked her.

She sighed as we walked down the corridor.

"I don't need a guide," I said. "I know where he is."

"Idiot, you're under guard."

"What do you think I'm going to do? Conquer you with sex, then take over? I can't fly this thing. I can't even start a new life. I don't have anything. I don't know anything!" My irritation surprised me but I also didn't care.

She finally acquiesced and answered me directly. "We had a meeting this morning, the crew, all of us. Just wait till you talk to him. Things are going to change."

The door to the captain's quarters opened and the familiar mess—boxes, parts of equipment, strewn clothes—from yesterday surrounded me. It was strangely calming to see the place again, the smell old leather, machine oils, cold coffee. The scents of a man. It was real here, lived in, less sterile than my quarters.

Slate stood by the desk, eyes moving over me as I entered, then turning away. He said nothing about the robe but I know he noticed it was closed today. Did it matter to him that it made me feel trapped, held down, pushed back? As if I were no one. As if I were an empty shadow he couldn't wait to be rid of.

I moved to the chair and sat without being asked, hearing the door close behind me.

"Feeling better today, huh?" Slate said.

"You have to let us out of our staterooms. We can help with things on the ship. We're not your enemies."

He nodded, going behind the desk and sitting. Today he wore a blue shirt, the leather vest, and blue jeans. Again, no boots.

"Well, if it's going to take longer for you to trust us, I'm out of that wine from my cupboard. I'll be wanting more." I kept telling myself I had reason to be grouchy. On Anada, I would never have given one thought to behaving this way. It would not have happened.

"Wine? Where did you get wine?"

My eyebrows rose. "It was in my stateroom. Two bottles. Good stuff, too."

"I didn't know about that. Must've been leftover from the person who occupied it before you. Well, there's rec rooms full of it. You can have all you want."

I sat up straighter. "Really?"

"Yeah." He waved his hand at me. "I'm going to rescind the lockdown. But your people have to pull their weight. And clothes, please."

My pulse livened. "I can't guarantee the clothes, but we'll do any jobs you give us. And if we don't know how, we'll learn."

"And you're all going to help us find you places to go."

I smiled. "Sell ourselves, you mean."

He inhaled deeply but did not answer.

"We can do that," I added.

"Well, hopefully you can do better than this." I saw a twinkle in his eye. He stood up and grabbed a tablet from the desk and brought it to me. I looked down.

"What am I looking at?" I asked.

"An ad."

Two naked humans, one male, one female, held a blue poster between them. On the poster were the words:

Made of Stardust and Mercury and the Whispers of Bridge World Winds
Rare Anadan Pleasure Slaves
Trained to Perfection
100% Submissive
Limited Supply
Discreet Shipment
Serious Bidders Only

"This ship was headed to the fringe worlds, Sector 818. The underworlds."

"Never heard of them," I said.

"Mostly the Empire ignores them, unless they need to buy or sell. Weapons, drugs, pleasure slaves. This was the ad the ship's former sales rep had created before we dropped in to visit." He flashed a quick grin. "Only the very wealthy or wealthy criminals could afford you. That was where you all were headed."

"There were thousands of us on Anada. Others of us would still be headed there."

"I didn't say we were going there," Slate corrected. "And if the Empire is smart, they probably planned to scatter you in groups to various underworlds throughout the galaxy. Sector 818 isn't the only seedy sector. Do you even realize how big the galaxy is?"

I remembered learning it. Slate might think I was a nobody, but I'd fight him on that at every turn. "Still largely unexplored, the estimate is over 400 billion stars, 100 billion planets. It's approximately 180,000 light years in diameter."

He looked down at me, hand out for the tablet. I put it back into his hand.

"Good," he said. "Then, smart ass, you know even in the explored sectors of the galaxy there are millions of places your people could be sold or abandoned or worse. So put them out of your mind."

I blinked up at him. "I wasn't thinking of a rescue effort. Just the 30 of us." I don't think I'd ever been called a smart ass before. Or called someone else one. I was tempted, though.

"Fine. Know this, too. If you betray any of us in any way, my crew and I will not only punish you, but your friends as well." He rolled his eyes. "I had to say that last part. My crew expects it."

"They don't know us. Yet." I gave him my most prim smile.

"Uh-huh. I'm sure that'll change."

I smirked at him.

"The prime job will be to find clients," he said. "Maybe you all can come up with some better ad copy for starters."

"So you'll be letting us do some work, then, kitchen or whatever's needed, too?"

"I don't run a military ship or schedule, Antares. Everyone does their own meals, or if they choose to eat in groups, they can do that. They clean up after themselves or leave a mess, do their own laundry or wear dirty clothes. Up to them. The ship runs itself but there are checks and balances to be done. I have people who know those ropes. So we don't really need technicians, which you are most definitely not. But we also don't need maids." He let out a partial laugh.

"That gives time for what we're really good at, I guess."

"Unfortunately."

I did not expect this reaction, and yet I did. He had already held me at arm's length for two days, as if he didn't trust me. Or himself. Maybe he had another lover. Or maybe he preferred women.

And me? I hadn't even tried to seduce him. What was wrong with me? That was usually how I got anything I wanted. And I hadn't had release in days. My libido usually demanded it. I was never intimidated by other men, but this one was different. I didn't want to fall to my knees for him. I wanted, instead, to know things about him. He intrigued me because I had never thought of having any kind of life like his. Because he was so different from me. How had he gotten where he was now? What made him a thief? And one capable of stealing an Empire starship? That was no small feat. Where did he come from? Was Slate his real name?

"Why do you say 'unfortunately'?" I challenged. "Pleasure is pleasure."

"You're whores. Different, yeah. Glorified. But still, you sell your pleasures. You're still whores."

"No, we're artists." I didn't normally take offense, so why was my chest hot?

"Say what you like."

"Artists sell their work, don't they? What's the difference? Just because it's pleasure?"

"Never had to pay for it myself." He fiddled with the tablet on the desk. "Not gonna start."

"In Anadan culture, it is the highest form of art." I added, before I could stop myself, "You get what you pay for."

He looked up and started to laugh. "You're really quick, aren't you? I won't underestimate you."

I met his dark eyes and held the gaze. "You shouldn't."

"All right, then. You want to go free your people?"

They weren't my people, but I couldn't get to his door fast enough.

Chapter Nine

How we would accomplish our plan was going to be a long, on-going effort. We were going to have to go to different planets, set up screening rooms, interviews. And all without attracting too much attention.

An Empire starship was no small thing that went unnoticed. But space was vast. We could dock at far distances in slide-space, untraced, and send a few people at a time on shuttles to meet and interview prospective clients.

We all learned to use the ship's computer system pretty quickly.

Slate contacted some of his sources where we were able to hook into private clubs, private organizations or high-end brothels so underground and elite that I wasn't sure who should be afraid of whom. People disappeared forever into those black holes. It didn't mean they were dead, but who could know?

The kinks out there did not disturb us. Some of us were experts at various so-called kinks. We were submissives, but we could take the whips in hand ourselves if asked. Clamps, ties, masks, humiliation, golden showers, fisting. Not much of that was my thing, but some of the others were not shy about it at all. The only rule we all shared: no murder fetishes. We were pleasure slaves. Not suicidal. Not into violence. And never the victim.

For hours a day, some of us searched, out of the millions that already existed in the galaxy, for planets and cultures that were most like Anada. They didn't exist. Or if they did, they were small and hidden. Out of the spotlight.

The crew grew used to us working by their sides without any clothing. Occasionally we wore our robes or straps of cloth that hid our genitals, mostly at meals if we took them with a group. And out of respect for Slate, who kept politely asking.

Slate had a natural leadership ability that was impressive. Whenever he came into a room, the energy level rose. His crew admired him. They were happy because he had made them rich, but also because he allowed self-expression while keeping everyone and everything in line. If there were any personal dramas, he took care to sort it out. If that meant talking or fighting it out, so be it. He allowed it. The rule was, once a confrontation occurred and ended, no more words would ever be spoken about it. If the problem recurred, one or both crewmembers would be asked to leave. I'd been told it had happened more than a few times.

The ship had five levels and three main recreation rooms. That did not count the small rec rooms, one on each level with an extra near the shuttle bay. These were more like resting rooms, or lunch rooms where the starguards could easily take a quick break.

More than once I walked into sexual orgies between Anadans and crew in some of these rooms. I felt right at home but I never joined in except for the one time that Amethyst and I were taken to on our first day here with the starguards.

Ocean became a particular star-in-the-making with the most requests for one of his "tricks" which he offered many times as an after dinner event for those interested in watching.

The trick? Ocean could beautifully and gracefully self-suck himself to orgasm. His long, limber body would move and bend just right to accomplish this. Others could manage, but not as well as Ocean. His gorgeous body, full pink lips and long, smooth cock made him the one to watch. Everyone came to at least one of his events, even Slate who would sit in a corner drinking from the bottle like the rogue he was and watch through slitted eyes.

But I never saw Slate join in any adult entertainment. I never saw him proposition anyone.

This increased his mystery. And my fascination with him. I wanted to know his deal. But I took it very slow. I engaged him in everything but sex in order to draw him out. He was an excellent backgammon player.

One night we were playing something called Interdimensional. It was a board game of many levels with marbles and other toys to move about in a complex series of strategies. It was so complicated we often had to look up the directions again and again. We fucked it up a lot and it made him laugh.

I liked when he laughed.

I took to wearing a loincloth when I knew I'd be around him. If I was completely naked, he would not look at me. So I compromised. I liked when he looked at me.

The crowd behind us was egging Ocean on, and I think another couple guys had joined him in the middle of the circle. They were all whistling and hooting, laughing and drinking. Having a generally good time. They were a wild bunch, a lot of fun, but often held back when Slate was around.

I mentioned this to him the first night we sat together.

"It's why I sit way over here," he told me. "I stay away a lot because I want them to have their fun. No surprise that they're more subdued when I'm around."

"The drawbacks of being the one in charge, I guess," I had said.

Right now we were focused on our game. Neither one of us even glanced at the antics of Ocean and the others. Sometimes we talked, and sometimes we were silent focusing completely on the game for ten or more minutes at a time.

Now Slate took a long sip of wine and looked at me across the weird sculpture of our triple board. "Why don't you ever join in the fun?" He nodded his head toward the crowd.

I smiled at him. Sometimes I teased him and he took it well, though he never invited me to his cabin. "Why? You want to see me attempt that feat?"

"Can you?"

I leaned back, bouncing a marble from one hand to the other. "Maybe I'll show you some day."

He laughed. Then his face relaxed. "Why are you different?"

"Different from what?"

"The others." He motioned toward the crowd again.

"I'm not. I am right at home with them."

He smiled, turned to the board, made a complex series of moves, and said, "You *are* different."

I said, "We all lost everything. We all deal with it in different ways. Maybe it just takes me longer to bounce back." I was not sure what was going on with me, but my words sounded almost right.

But then there was the unanswered question of my libido, and why I wasn't as tuned in to it as much anymore. That was all chemical, a permanent conditioning I'd had in the harem. Grief might have affected it. I hadn't cried. Maybe this was my way. I'd masturbated only once during the entire week. For me, for my kind, that was unheard of. And when I'd done it, the whole time I'd thought of Slate. Not naked, no. But imagining him standing before me in that skirted black jacket over his puffiest white shirt, and wearing those boots with the ridges, like the back of a dragon. Behind him, the star fields pulsed. Then the stars descended upon him, in his hair, on his coat, flickering against his face. The whites of his eyes glowed. But that gaze. That gaze was deep and dark; a sadness wavered there. I could feel it all about me. After I came, I felt so strange, as if a shadowed wind had left its essence upon me.

"I'm sorry for that, Antares. The Empire takes. It's a force no one can reckon with. Why do you think I live the way I do?"

"I have wondered what made you go into this way of life."

"I started out as a pickpocket."

"How old were you?"

"14."

"You had family, though, right?"

Something dulled in his eyes, but he said, simply, "Yes." He took another drink.

"And now it's starships."

He shrugged as if it were no big deal.

The crowd hooted. It must've been something good. But then again, they were all supremely drunk.

Ignoring them, I said, "What's the grandest thing you ever stole?"

"Hmm. Other than a starship, well it would have to be that kiss I stole from Mary Fourfivesix when I was five."

Now he was making me laugh. "What kind of name is Fourfivesix?"

"I always thought maybe there were 456 Marys in her family."

"Oh, that wasn't her last name?"

He shook his head no.

I said, "My first kiss was a girl, too, though I prefer boys. Her name was Pumpkin."

He busted out laughing again. "Pumpkin?"

"I swear on the holy priapus of my forefathers. Would I lie about something like Pumpkin?"

He was laughing so hard now, I wasn't sure he heard that last. But then he said, between breaths, "Holy priapus?" And started all over again.

I crossed my arms. "Hey, it's not funny to make light of someone's religion."

"Oh, I'm not. I'm not." But he shook all over.

68

I got up, went over to the storage unit, and grabbed another bottle of wine. I opened it, then brought it over to the game table. He was still wiping his eyes.

The crowd was still noisy, but a little more subdued now. Maybe the guys were taking breaks before another round.

I poured the fresh wine all the way to the brims of our glasses. I winked at him. He was still laughing. "I don't think we've had enough of this yet," I said.

Of course that set him off again.

I lifted my glass to him. "Drink up."

When the crowd dispersed, we barely noticed. Trying to figure out this complicated game had become an obsession for two drunken men. When we left the room I don't even know how late it was. We had had that good of a time together.

I woke in the morning slightly hung over and regretting that once again I had not pushed myself at him. Yet what we had was nice, the games, the companionship. I really enjoyed being with him and my mind told me not to complicate it further.

But the whole morning I was frustrated. I sat at the computer and did nothing.

The more I held back from Slate, the more I wanted him. I had no idea why this was a problem for me. Sexually I had no inhibitions. I gave my confidence no second thoughts. When it came to Slate, then, why did I freeze?

If I'd invited him to my bed, even if he'd said "no" I would've been fine with it. Everyone has a choice. It didn't matter to me. But with Slate it did matter. For the first time in my life, I was afraid. Of another person. Of not being good enough. Of rejection.

When I looked in the mirror, now, I'd smack my palm against my forehead. I took long baths. I stayed away from the computer as much as possible.

And at night Slate and I would play our games. Drink wine. Ignore all the sex that was going on around us.

One night, the game sculpture between us, Slate said to me, "Your people are working out."

I glanced up from where I was contemplating a move. "They're not really my people."

"Some of them already have prospects for new owners and we're already setting up a schedule. Some have as many as three on their 'wish lists'."

"That's good." I moved, sitting back with a sense of accomplishment.

"So what about you?"

"What about me?"

"Your 'wish list'. How's it coming along?"

"Nothing yet." I couldn't look at him when talking about this subject, so I studied the game again.

"Not even any remote possibilities? An interest, even?"

I took a deep breath. "Nope."

Tonight the rec room was quiet. Maybe they'd all gone off to one of the other break rooms, tired of our shadows in the corner intruding upon their scene.

"Why not?"

I didn't want to talk to him. Not about this. "I chose my profession, you know."

"You told me that." He was staring at me, dark, unnerving. But I loved his eyes. Any time he looked at me, my stomach would jump.

"I went into the harem to train in this area of Anadan culture because I loved the aspect of it. To me, my potential owners weren't strangers. I knew what to expect, every angle. I did it because I love pleasure, giving pleasure, receiving pleasure, learning to do it well, be the best. That was not just my skill, it was my heart, my culture. It's all gone now." Saying the words out loud brought a wave of grief. "The outside worlds are so alien. Nothing out there matches up to what I had."

70

"Nothing?" His voice was gentle, low.

I sighed but did not answer. Everything seemed chaotic in my mind. I could barely begin to put that into words.

"It's your art. You said so yourself."

"Well, maybe I have other arts in me, too. Painting. Gardening." I gestured at the bulkhead. "Flying starships. Maybe I'm some great poet and I don't even know it yet." I stood up, suddenly uncomfortable, needing to move. "Have you always been a thief? A criminal? Is that all you ever wanted?" I turned toward the cupboard of wine, but didn't get any out. I stood there for a moment, wondering why I was suddenly shaking. There was a burning pain in my chest. I was so defensive. So *lost*!

Slate said, never moving from the table but obviously sensing my discomfort, "Antares. I'm sorry the Empire came to your world. It's shit. It is."

Laid bare now with just those words, out in the open, all of it became so real now. I'd bottled up my grief. I'd tried to ignore the bigger picture and distract myself. Not think about the future at all. Ironically, it was all a lot easier when I thought I was going to die.

I bowed my head. My eyes got so hot so fast I couldn't stop it. The heat of my grief stung my face. In seconds tears dripped down my cheeks, jaw, chin.

Now I heard him move. He was wearing those amazing boots tonight. They clomped across the floor. I could smell the leather, and the precious salts of his skin. His heat behind me felt like it could make my skin curl. When his hand touched the center of my naked back I leaned forward. Not to get away from it, but because the counter was there and I thought I might fall. My knees were shaking. I wasn't sure they would support me.

As I bowed my head into my upturned hands, his palm stayed still against my back. He said nothing. Very slowly, his palm moved in a small circle. I couldn't breathe. I could only stand there and feel more tears crawling down my face.

71

Furious at myself, I tried to wipe them away but there was too much dampness.

The two of us stood there in the garish white light because there was nothing else to do, nowhere else to go. I thought I should explain myself. That I was really okay, it all just been a very long road to get this far. It was my way to not involve others in my feelings, make light of my own moods which, in the scope of things, weren't important when compared to getting problems solved. But I couldn't speak. My voice was gone.

Finally, I straightened, though the tears still fell.

Slate's hand moved slowly down my side. "Fuck, but your skin is soft," he whispered.

I gasped in surprise at his words. It was a compliment I was used to, but from him it did the job of jolting me, instantly distracting my sadness.

The far wall was a two-way monitor. A star meadow glimmered upon it. I made myself stare at it, made myself not think of anything at all except the touch of his hand on my waist, and his so delightful words.

The lights of the stars blurred like gold explosions through my tears. My heart seemed to cramp up. Everything about me was cramped. If I could just merge myself with that view. Settle down in a beam of light and travel forever maybe, just maybe, that would be enough.

He remained firm, standing behind me. I wanted the attention turned off of myself and onto him.

"So." I bent my head, letting him see my tears now. "How did you steal this ship? I never asked you that. Where did all the starguards go? Did you kill them?"

His hand fell to his side. He leaned his hip against the counter as if everything were normal and he wasn't looking at a miserable guy who'd just broken open before him, and began to speak. "A viral malfunction. Not real, of course."

I sniffed. "What is the viral malfunction you used?" I wiped the back of my hand across my cheeks.

"You set the ship on self-destruct mode. A computer virus does it remotely, actually."

I nodded, understanding. "You made them think they had to vacate the ship."

"Didn't you notice all but one shuttle is gone?"

"Why'd they leave that one?"

He grinned, casually reaching up and brushing at the moisture on my face. My heart nearly stopped.

"Another malfunction," he said. "When they tried to move the shuttle, it didn't work. I had to make sure they left one behind for us. You never can be sure. You can't have a ship without lifeboats. That's like diving straight into the face of fate."

"So they all just left? Left it behind?"

"They got out fast. The computer told them the explosion was unforeseen and immediate. It would make the space here hot for a long time. They weren't going to stick around."

"And then you boarded." This was just what I needed, to focus on something separate from myself. Someone else's story.

"Yep. They took off fast. Kane's our virus specialist. He's a master with that stuff, actually. The Empire has outstanding technology, so he had to breech a lot of doors. Took him nine months to write and test his program. I guess he's sort of a genius, like you and your skill."

I frowned. "But I'm just a whore, you said."

"Yeah. I said that, didn't I?"

I nodded. "But I wasn't offended. On my world it's not a bad word."

He didn't laugh. If possible, his eyes turned sad. "Well, on my world it was. It shouldn't have been, but it was." He glanced around as if suddenly nervous, then he put his hand against the side of my head, fingertips sinking into my braided hair, and said, "Antares, I really am sorry this happened to you. It shouldn't have. There are some things that—that just should never happen."

I knew then that he was referring to something in his own past. I wanted to know about that. I wanted to know everything about him. "Thank you."

He rubbed my arm, his eyebrows narrowing. "How does your skin get so soft?"

I started to laugh and the tears and everything else no longer mattered in this moment. "That's what you want to know?"

"Imminently!" He laughed.

"It's a process. A lot of different things that change the taste of it, the scent. It gets rid of all the hair, too. From the neck down. A combination of potions and baths. Repeated for a period of time."

I watched as his Adam's apple bobbed. He swallowed again. My breath caught in the back of my throat. His hand came forward, cupping my still-damp cheek. His eyes were a lighter brown up close, framed by thick lashes as glossy as outer space. He leaned forward, bent his head and kissed me very lightly on the forehead, then moved slowly down, his lips trailing over my eyebrows, the bridge of my nose, down the side of one cheek. When his mouth touched mine the skin all over my body instantly flushed. I put my hand against his leather vest and that was it. This was what I'd wanted. Since I first saw him. Since he first stepped boldly into the cargo hold and realized he'd found treasure worth more than the starship he'd just stolen.

This pirate had made a fortune taking everything he wanted. I wanted to know everything about him.

He pulled back and whispered, "Is it okay? Are you okay?"

"Okay," I breathed, watching as his pupils dilated, as he finally showed me he wanted me.

He gestured toward the couch by the monitor-wall. "By the stars?" he asked.

74

I shook my head. "No. In your room."

"My room's a mess."

I smiled at him. "I love how it smells."

"You're crazy." His laugh accompanied his second kiss. My mouth parted to accept it.

I leaned back and took his hand in mine. "Please?"

"Yes."

Chapter Ten

I led him out the door and down the white corridor. His heavy boots clomped against the deck. He smelled earthy and male. His hand clasped mine tightly. He walked obediently behind me, but he was no passive follower.

I felt my cock bob beneath the silk cloth at my crotch.

His tight jeans must've been constricting him.

Before we got to his door, he pulled me back. I let him take me into his arms. He pressed me up against the bulkhead and kissed me again.

Turning my head to the side, I said, "Can't wait?"

He shook his head. "No."

"Your door's five feet away."

"Fuck it." He kissed me again, pushing himself against me. I loved the weight. I wanted more. But inside. Where he lived. Amid all his things. His flavors and scents. The clothes he wore. The sheets his body touched, where his breath flowed, where he slept.

I broke away. A whisper. Soft. "Come on." I took his hand in mine. He stumbled behind me and into his room.

As he had said, it was a mess and I loved it. All the imperfections were just so... perfect. We waded through scattered clothing and tablets, rumpled papers and machine parts. I'd never asked him what all that was. Now, I didn't care.

Humans had been colonizing the known galaxy for thousands of years. But their hearts and souls were still contained in private rooms filled with the colors and textures and fragrances of the things they loved.

The rumpled bed was cast in shadow as his hand brushed the wall where the lights were controlled.

"Lower," I said. "But still enough to see."

I liked the dimness, on the edge of night, but with enough glow to see details. I wanted to look into his eyes again. I wanted to watch the blush darken him, spread across his olive skin.

I sat on the edge of his bed, arms open and held up as he came into them. We fell back, the leather vest against my cheek, the gray sheets pressed to my back, my braid caught behind my shoulder. His weight encompassed me. Everything in me surged upwards.

We kissed, twisting against each other, my arms holding him tight, moving under his vest, hands feeling the muscles of his back. He had tight musculature, broad shoulders, narrow waist and hips.

The kisses seemed rushed at first, but in reality we couldn't stop. Couldn't move on because we were basking in them. For a long time it was just that, the clinging of bodies, the affection in that simple meeting of lips, tongues.

When we could stand no more, we began to roam with other body parts in other areas. I pushed his leather jacket over his shoulders and down. He flung it to the deck. My hands invaded his white shirt. He helped me unbutton it. When it slid to his waist I was gifted with a magnificence of medium brown skin, taut at the curves where small, dark brown nipples puckered at exposure to the air. I ran my hands up and down his smooth chest. A dusting of dark hair, fine and short, spread above his pecs. My fingertips trickled down his ribs. He sat back to let me undo his jeans.

Our arms tangled up for a moment when he kept reaching out to stroke my own heaving chest. "Up," I whispered, and he lifted himself from my thighs as I pushed the pants over his hips and down. He had on black underwear and that came down, too. I pushed everything down as his beautiful cock sprang free. But the boots stopped us from going any further.

Those thick, ridged, sexy, knee-length boots.

I pushed him back and to the side, then scurried down to his legs and feet. My hands ran up and down the polished leather. He stayed still, though his lovely, erect cock bobbed, and let me explore the boots. They were finely made. Terribly ostentatious. And so 'him'.

A hidden recess beneath a leather flap showed me they buttoned down the sides. The buttons were round, like shiny copper coins. I undid first the left boot, then the right. I carefully pulled each one from his feet. Then I set them gently on the deck below the foot of the bed. Their cloying, rich smell was all over my hands now.

When I lay back down beside Slate, he stretched alongside me and helped me get his pants down over his feet. He kicked them to the floor. Then he began to paw the silks at my crotch.

"Here," I said. I showed him how the material was merely wrapped about my emerald studded belt. He yanked it free in front. My exposed cock, jutting from the ring, pointed toward my stomach.

He gently touched the diamond-glittered ring but not my skin. "Do you want to keep that?"

"I feel like it's part of me," I said. "Like this is for you." I touched the chains of the slave-bracelet at his wrist. I could tell he never took it off.

"Okay." He reached underneath me, hands brushing my backside, and pulled the silk from the back of the belt. I lifted up and he tossed the fluttering, colorful scarf to the side.

He was breathing heavily, sighing as he looked at me. I rolled and pulled him against me. Our bodies met, our erections trapped between our bellies. We undulated together. I bent my head over him and kissed him.

We were on our sides, one hand each trapped. But Slate's free hand moved over my waist and the belt, down my hip and over my buttocks. He caressed me that way over and over, sighing into my mouth.

My free hand moved back and forth across his back. Our legs wove together.

Somewhere worlds were ending. In this room, flame ruled.

I was so hot. I wanted him all over me, his skin, his breath, his mouth, his essence. I wanted to lick him everywhere, taste every bit of him. Pet. Caress. Fondle.

Slowly we moved to new stages. Our legs spread. We came apart with room enough to nuzzle, stretch, navigate each other's territory.

We were careful, both so on edge. Unspoken, we had an agreement that we wanted this to last. But I also thought, *We have all night*. I was quite sure we'd rile each other up again and again. But this first time—oh, this first time would never come again.

He had his back to me, bent to caress my thighs.

I had never seen Slate without his clothing before. His naked back was covered in flowers. Not literally. They were inked into his skin, delicate, colorful, little lacy membranes of cascading bouquets.

"You have flowers on your back," I said. I gave a little yell as his arm chafed lightly, as if by accident, over my cock.

"I got that tat when I was eighteen." His breath puffed warm on my inner thigh, moving up.

I moved my hands over an array of colors that rippled under his muscles. "It's gorgeous."

Some of the flowers had little tentacles. Others, barbs or thorns. The petals ranged over his shoulders in scarlet, orange, lavender, blue. A wild field of spring blooms.

"I don't get to see it." Breath warm on my aching cock now. "But I'm the one who drew that. I took it to a girl who did the tat."

"You're an artist!"

His chuckled filled the room. "I'm a thief."

"But—but, it's wonderful… um!"

His tongue touched the tip of my cock. My hand slipped down over the tat, the skin; my head fell back.

He nuzzled me, licked, lightly suckled. Echo of water lapping at a shore, pulling back.

Astonished at my lack of control, I hung on just a tendril of that sound.

The hour thinned. Time unweaved. Air of groans. My dark sylph.

Somehow he kept me from coming and we switched places. Teasing each other to the brink, pulling back. We weren't virgins, but it felt so close to that. I took extra care. Drew things out.

His cock had a beautiful pinkness at the tip that I loved, joining gracefully to a dark shaft. He tasted of hot burning coals, and autumn spice. He moaned low in his throat, his breaths heavy and strained.

Soon urgency would not be denied.

"Come here," he said, pulling at my curled legs, forcing them to spread.

I did not want to let go of his cock. My mouth watered all around it.

"Gods!" he cried, unable to keep from thrusting. He grabbed my hips, pulling me down until we were in the sixty-nine position, and I felt myself engulfed in an eager, damp mouth.

I sucked at him harder. Sounds of pleasure filled the captain's stateroom.

I could not hold back. Everything inside me surrendered to pure pleasure, to this moment, to him. My cock pulsed as I felt him let go as well, filling my mouth with his ecstasy, his essence.

*

Staring at the bedroom ceiling, there was a goldness on the air. And all over me.

Even now, his slightest breath over my skin made it flush.

I could tell Slate was not asleep.

I said to him, "Why did you never look at me those first days?"

"I did look at you."

"You always looked away."

"Because you are so beautiful, more than any of the others. You were so distracting. More outspoken than the others. I didn't know you and I still wasn't sure."

"Sure about what?"

"Everything. Anything. All of it. This." His fingertips made intricate designs against my lower back.

I smiled and drifted.

I must've dozed because I woke to him kissing me and everything was renewed, my blood rushing, my cock hard. Skin on skin, slick and heated. Lips, tongue, a velvet luxury.

I wrapped my arms and legs around him and he gasped my name. There were more endearments, lots of rubbing, licking. Kisses along my chest, my ribs until he turned me and planted them all down my spine. He tentatively licked at a dimple above my buttocks. I lifted them to him and he began to knead and stroke them, with bolder caresses going in between.

I turned my head to look at him. "You can if you want to."

He said absently, "What?"

"Fuck me."

And now the air was made of sighs. He licked me until I was dripping. Probed with gentle fingers until I squirmed.

So polite, he felt my cock to make sure I was hard as he moved over me, as he put one arm around my chest and pulled me up. I wanted to beg, but I stayed silent.

When he pushed in, it felt like every door inside me opened. I forgot about those harem spring-days and thought only of the night, moonlit across all the sleeping souls of all the galaxies. My skin was caressed by bright darkness lapping, and everything dawned fresh and new. Yet also deep and ancient. Endless mystery. The fathoms of him.

After awhile, I said, "Turn me over. I want to face you."

He pulled out, helped me turn and spread my legs. He plunged into me again and I hung onto his shoulders for dear life.

A litany began in my mind, silent stars flaring in my heart, on my skin. His voice. His voice carrying me away on a beam of light. Saying my name over and over. He broke the molds of all my finest fantasies. Tears of pleasure slid along my temples.

We both came, our yells no doubt echoing throughout the ship.

*

We took a shower together and later dozed again, only to wake and realize we still could not keep our hands to ourselves. Or our mouths.

He kissed me hungrily. "You taste like cake and ice cream."

I laughed. "More," I murmured under his tongue.

He licked all the way down my body, my cock finding its way into his mouth again.

The air became pink and heavy.

*

I'm a perfectionist. But Slate made me sloppy. Made me lose focus.

When I awoke the next day I felt lost. It took me a moment to orient. I lay in Slate's bed alone. Sitting up, I looked around for him. I saw his boots were missing. His clothes which he'd tossed to the floor the night before were also gone.

I listened for sounds of him in his office area. Nothing.

Slowly, I got up and went into the bathroom. After a nice shower, I re-braided my hair, re-attached the silk to my emerald belt, and went in search of food.

I could find Slate nowhere.

After asking around, I discovered he was down in engineering. "Something about a lighting glitch, he said," Kane told me. "I don't know. I only know computers. Not that shit."

The thrum of the starship, its beating heart, lived down on the engineering level. As I walked along the corridors, the shadows ghosted around me. The lighting was golden here. A dim twilight.

I checked room after room. No Slate.

Finally, at the end of the hall I turned and saw him sitting on the floor surrounded by pieces of equipment and a part of the bulkhead was missing.

I stood for awhile to see if he'd notice me, but his head was bent, intent on the innards of something, a strange tool in his left hand. He wore yesterday's jeans, a clean cotton pullover shirt, red with long sleeves and buttons at the throat, and his black vest. His beautiful hair was slicked back in its tail again. It reflected the bronze shades of the room.

"What are you doing?" My voice seemed to ring too loud through the room.

Slate looked up. "Antares."

"When did you leave? This morning, I mean."

"It was late. But I wanted to let you sleep. So I was quiet."

I nodded. "Are you okay?"

"Perfectly."

"Is something wrong with the ship?"

He glanced around at his mess. He sat almost cross-legged in the middle of it, his big boots making it impossible to look really comfortable. They crossed at the ankles and Slate leaned his back against the open bulkhead. "Oh, I know this might look bad but actually it's a glitch I've been wanting to check out for awhile now."

I came over and sat down next to him. "Even with the thrumming of the ship, it's peaceful down here. Maybe it's because of the noise. Like a big purring cat."

"Yeah." He looked back at whatever that thing was in his hand. It had a burnt oil smell.

"Hey," I said. "You know you can talk to me. About anything. About last night."

"Everything's fine." He smiled at me and went back to work.

"Do you need anything? Lunch maybe?"

"No, I'm fine."

"I can bring you something."

"I'm all right. Really. This is just something I needed to get done. I have a list."

"I know that," I said gently. "And it really is peaceful down here."

"Yeah."

Sighing, I rose. "I'll leave you to it, then. Do you want to come up and have coffee or dinner later?"

"Sure." But he did not reach out to me. He did not try to touch me.

"Okay. Later."

I walked slowly back the way I'd come, the shadow-ghosts of engineering trailing behind me.

My training did not only include physical pleasure. Back in my harem days, I also learned of the endless psychologies of pleasure, how the various chemicals released could make people react in all different ways and all different extremes, from feelings of outright falling in love to merely cool affection bordering on indifference.

I knew Slate was not indifferent. But I also knew he was probably feeling things he wanted time to process. So was I. So there was a good side to his behavior.

But still, as I emerged from engineering to the upper decks, my breath came shallow. My hands shook.

I pretended to work the rest of the afternoon. I sat in front of a computer in the main rec room looking busy. No one bothered me. No one even knew Slate and I had spent the night together. They were used to me being the quiet one, now.

Hours went by.

The room filled with some of the crew and Anadans. They liked to play games there, eat there, watch vids. And of course there were those famous nights a few times a week when Ocean, and sometimes others, would put on quite a show.

I put my computer away.

Dusk and I played a vid together. If he noticed I was quieter than usual, he didn't ask.

At long last I saw Slate enter. His shining hair was still pulled back in a small tail. It reflected all the colors of the room. He had changed his shirt. The white one again. It was undone at the neck revealing the shadow of hair there. He still wore those enthralling boots. He came straight over to me. "Have you eaten?"

I shook my head.

Even though we were in the middle of our game, Dusk said, "Go on."

I got up and we went to the galley and found all sorts of good stuff to pile on our plates.

Finally, Slate grinned at me. "Worked up an appetite, I guess."

I grinned back.

We took the food, and a bottle of wine from some deeper recess in the galley I had never noticed before. We carried it all back to the rec room to our usual corner table and feasted on chicken, rice, garlic bread and wine. Oranges and ice cream made up our dessert.

The Empire stocked its starships for long voyages, so we had plenty of supplies. Food filled the galley holds nearly to the ceiling. We would not starve before having to re-supply for a long, long time.

"So did you fix the glitch?" I asked, in between bites.

"I think so."

"Well," I said, "now I've seen engineering. Any chance I can see the bridge some time?"

"It's all auto, mostly off-limits except in emergency or when a new course comes up. But sure. As long as you're not planning a mutiny or something."

I gave him a reproachful look. "Is it just like a computer room?"

"Pretty much."

"Oh. Sounds pretty boring."

When we were finished, I said, "So, you want to play a game or something?"

"I was thinking of turning in early," he replied, standing to clear his plate.

"Oh."

He looked down at me as he gathered up my plate as well. "Coming?" He gave me a quick wink.

Just that one word, and the wink, and my skin instantly heated. "Sure."

I got up and followed him out the door.

Chapter Eleven

We were on the bed and naked pretty quick. And it started all over again, just like last night.

I loved the touch of him, the smells. His hands all over me sent me into spirals of ecstasy.

We made love slowly at first, like before, then sped up.

I had my hand under his strong thigh, cupping one buttock. His skin was like flame. My other hand pressed down on his hip and his cock jutted straight up. I lowered my mouth on it, craving the taste, loving how he shuddered and moaned, thrilled that it was me doing this to him and no one else.

His balls were drawn up, and I nipped and licked at them as well. Knowing I could make him so hard and tight gave me as much pleasure as it did him. I rubbed the smooth skin of his stomach, gripped his ass. Sucked all the delicious moisture from his cock until he begged me to stop.

I came up and kissed him delicately, letting him get a small taste of himself. He put his arms around me and held me, kissing me all over my face.

"Antares," he said, "what are you doing to me?"

I pulled the tie from his hair and ran my hands through it. So silken. "I don't know. What am I doing to you?"

He moved over my body and used his hands and mouth to bring me to aching completion. It was so wonderful, different from anything I'd felt before. Perfection in every imperfection—for he was not a trained pleasure slave and yet he was better than anyone I'd ever had—and me completely out of control. With him, my body responded in ecstasy, but instead of being sated, my hunger for him only increased after every orgasm, every encounter.

As we lay catching our breaths in each other's arms, I said, "I want to know everything about you."

He laughed. "Everything might take awhile."

"Okay." I kissed the tangled of hair at the edge of his temple. "I already know you were a pickpocket at age 14."

"Yeah. And things just grew from there."

"I'll bet you have some adventures to tell."

He propped himself up on his elbow. "What about you? Of course you have wild stories of your own. Antares the sex slave. Your indoctrination stories at 18 alone could probably keep me going if I were stranded on an ice moon for an entire winter season."

"Maybe. But I want to know about you. When you were 14, were you alone? What happened to you?"

"Ah, well, some of it was on the streets. A harsh place to grow up fast. I tried to stay off 'em as much as possible. So much crime. Drugs. Prostitution. Rape. Murder. Not good stories for a kid to overhear. Or witness."

I looked up at him, my eyebrows narrowed. "I'm sorry. You witnessed these crimes?"

"Sometimes."

I heard his voice grow distant. To bring him back into focusing on me, I said, "On Anada there was no crime like that. For that I was lucky."

The moisture in Slate's eyes shifted, giving him a still-faraway look. "But there's slavery."

"Not in the sense that you're using that word."

"No?"

I shook my head. "We have a voice. Rules. All of us are consenting."

"But what about the secrets in the shadows. The slaves you never hear about."

"It wasn't like that." How to explain to someone who'd only ever seen the dark sides of things? Of this?

"You were only 24 when you left. Much younger when you trained. Sheltered, obviously. What would you know about it?"

"I would've heard stories. We were a very open community."

"And now me and my crew, with you all helping, are selling you and your friends all over again. An underworld trade. The particular area of seediness I worked hard to avoid."

I bit hard on my lower lip. Selling me, he had said. He could not know I had done no work toward that goal. But the worst part was he said it as if it were going to happen and he didn't expect anything else from me. A given. And of course that was what would happen. How could I not want an owner? I'd trained for that all my life. I'd excelled at my art. It was what I lived for.

"But if it's what they—we want, our art, then there is a choice. It's our choice." Why was I being defensive?

"Your art. Your choice." His mouth muscles went rigid. "So said some of the people I knew when I was a kid. They sold themselves for drugs, food, a roof. Because that's what they wanted, they said. They thought they had no other skills. They thought—" He stopped. His mouth turned down.

I said, gently, "How are you a victim when you're a consenting adult?"

He sat up against the pillows, drawing the sheet to his waist. "Because of how you are treated and seen. Because of how you are used. *That* you are used."

"It's a mindset."

"Oh?"

I sat up next to him. Our shoulders and hips touched. Our ankles were crossed. His skin radiated warmth against mine. "Well, for example, some starguards took me and Amethyst away that first day. To the shuttle bay rec room."

"What?"

"They were tempted by us, of course. As pleasure slaves we expect that. They had ideas on their minds, naturally."

"Fucking bastards. If they didn't ask you, it was rape on their minds."

"No. We were perfectly willing."

"But they just took you?"

"Yes."

"Antares, don't you realize even if you were willing that they were using you?"

"Yes. But what they wanted we could easily give. It's what we do best."

"But it wasn't your choice. You didn't get a say."

"But we were fine with them. Everything was under our control."

"That's an illusion, don't you see?"

I shook my head but my mind went strangely quiet when he asked, "Were you allowed to say 'no'?"

On my home world there were no victims, only consenting adults. And we were allowed to say 'no' even to our masters if we weren't feeling well, if there was some other problem. If things got too complicated mediators came in. Pleasure slaves had a voice. We lived in a safe environment. All of us.

With all of that taken away, now everything was just a mass of confusion.

"In your life were you ever really able to say 'no'?" he asked.

"Of course!" My voice came out strangled, annoyed. What could he understand? He'd never lived it. He didn't come from my culture. He came from one where people like me were no better than trash fluttering in the gutter. I was the devil in a whirlwind of filth. 'Whore' was a bad word to his people. What I was to him: Less than human.

I wanted to explain. But there is a flaw in all people. I've seen it play out over and over. They think if only they can explain themselves better the rest of the world will finally understand, fall to its knees, accept them.

How could I expect someone to understand pleasure slavery who had never been raised in the culture of it, let alone trained to it?

"Have you ever said 'no'?" he asked.

If 'whore' were a bad word to him and he thought of me as that, this conversation was going too far. I put my hand in the center of his chest and said, "I could have at any time. My choice. The end."

But he did not let the conversation rest. "Then your answer is you have not. Because you are trained not to."

"Slate." Had he even heard me when I said we have a voice? Or perhaps he thought I was lying.

He looked away. "And with me, I'm one more person you can't say 'no' to."

The clarity of this conversation came to me in a flash. I could not win no matter what I said. I took a deep breath. I said his name again. But he would not look at me.

I let my hand fall to his side. We sat side by side, unmoving. I couldn't think what to say. If my very nature was despicable to him, then had we shared a lie for the last two nights? My mind would not accept that. Nor my heart.

"What does is matter," I said softly, "who does what, or their reasons, with as many partners as they wish, if it's consenting?"

I could hear his breath. See his beautiful chest rise and fall. Then I heard him whisper. "Maybe you should leave."

"I don't want to leave."

"But I want you to."

I reached out, touching his shoulder. "But this, what we have, it's—"

Before I could finish he pushed my hand away.

I raised myself up to look at him. "I have a voice."

"Huh." He looked straight at me. "Not in this world you don't."

"That's not quite fair." I reached out to him again, and again he shoved my arm. This time it was a harder push and I wasn't prepared for his strength. It was all so surreal. I went over the edge of the bed and hit the floor on my side before I even knew I was falling. I knew he didn't mean to do that. He was simply pushing my arm away. But when I looked around at where I sat on the floor, I saw all the junk, and me, the newest item. Something to be thrown on the floor like his discarded clothes and toys.

Even more infuriating, he did not bother to check on me to see if I'd been injured. I wasn't, but the shock of his strength and the fall hurt. For a moment I couldn't breathe. And something in my chest was cracking open spilling everything, all my emotions, my pain, and my love down some invisible drain. I saw my silk scarf draped over a discarded metal tube. I reached for it and my knee hit a sharp metal object. Tears smarted in my eyes. I'd be damned if I'd let him see them.

I grabbed up my scarf and stood. I moved toward the door and never looked back.

Chapter Twelve

I never saw the corridor. I moved by instinct alone. I found myself, arms up, pushing forward on Dusk and Nile's door. I might've gone to Ocean and Amethyst for comfort, but they were cool, always cool. Our whole family had been that way, possibly me the coldest of all. But now I needed warmth, wanted to see love between two people that was real. I needed that rare treasure.

The door opened and Nile stood naked in dim coppery light.

"Antares! Hey. Dusk is still in the rec room if you're looking for him."

"Can I just come in? I don't want to be alone right now."

"Of course!" He stood to the side.

I knew he would welcome me. It was the Anadan way. I saw his and Dusk's rumpled bed and headed for it, flopping face forward onto the mattress.

"Antares, what's wrong?"

I pulled a pillow to my face, smelling the honey and spice of the two pleasure slave lovers, and tried not to cry. I was so angry. But more, the pains in my heart pierced like knives. I turned my head. "I feel like I'm having a heart attack."

I saw Nile come around the bed, felt him beside me as he sat, his soft hand stroking my back. He said, "Hey, whatever it is, we'll get through it. We've all gotten this far together under the worst conditions. Utter destruction. We've all had it hard." He continued to stroke me and talk to me. He asked me if I missed my owner. I did, of course. I'd had safety and a family, but I've never been in love with him. Or Ocean. Or Amethyst. Still, all the changes were like a crash. And this one last drama, after my heart might be just beginning to mend, was too much.

I realized since the invasion of the Empire, I'd been very alone. I hadn't sought comfort from anyone. Until now, I wasn't aware of how withdrawn I'd been.

Finally, Nile said, "Is it something to do with you and Slate?"

I turned my head from the pillow and stared at him. "What do you mean?"

"Well, everyone knows you two have been, well, spending time together."

"Yeah. So?"

"Well, we all figured you were sleeping together."

"What?"

"Yeah. You have been sleeping with him, haven't you? I mean, seducing the top guy. Pure genius on your part. You always were my best teacher, you know."

"No. We weren't sleeping together. I mean not until last night."

"Oh." His perfectly trimmed eyebrows narrowed. "Really? Because we thought it had been going on for, well, weeks. Everyone just sort of assumed it, I guess."

I grimaced and put my face back onto the pillow.

"Did Slate do something? Are you hurt?" Nile asked. His hand touched the back of my neck.

My eyes heated. I turned into the pillow. It was as if I were a kid again and everything was out of my control.

When Nile couldn't get me to talk further, he simply lay down next to me and put his arms around me. His ultra-soft skin felt so natural. Only another Anadan could understand me so well. I turned into his arms and let him hold me as my mind went into a kind of daze. I didn't want to think. I just wanted to float away from it all, the stars streaming beyond me.

When Dusk came in and found us together, he didn't say any word of protest. He brought me some water and held me close. I almost started to cry again, fighting the fierce hot tears, wiping angrily at my eyes. The two of them stroked my head and back, then lay down with me sandwiched between them.

My eyes were tightly closed. My breathing came in fits and starts.

"Hush, Antares," Dusk said just before I fell to sleep. "We've all gone through this terrible, terrible disaster. And missing our loved ones." He kissed my cheek. "We'll take care of you."

Their satiny bodies surrounded me. Grounded me through the ship's night cycle. I could not have had better friends.

*

During the night and a fitful sleep, memory took me back to harem lessons on love.

We sat naked on velvet pillows, a trainer to the left of each one of us. This was less a lovemaking class and more about science. The science of sex.

We all nicknamed the class mathsex, and often groaned out loud when required to attend.

As pleasure slaves, technique was always stressed, but knowing that the brain produces different chemicals for feelings of pleasure, satisfaction, supreme ecstasy and the ultimate indefinable experience, love, was drummed into us. Knowing these things, combined with our skills in sexual gratification better equipped us to deal with varying degrees of emotions we could encounter in our owners and our other acquaintances: brother and sister slaves, grooms, trainers.

Today we had halos on our heads that took pictures of, and measured our brain activity as we went through various stages of arousal. By understanding our own brain's reactions, we could learn better empathy, sympathy and compassion for potential partners and ourselves. In other words, this class was to help with maturity at dealing with relationships at all levels of intimacy.

Today I had Sol for my trainer. He was one of my favorites, always patient with me. His smile made me relaxed and comfortable. I never felt that anything I did was wrong when I was with him. He could be strict with me while reaffirming. With other trainers, I often burst into tears. I was only 18 and everything was still so new to me. But Sol aroused me like none of the others and I was eager to please him in any way.

Sol had soft white hair cut short and spiky. His eyes were my favorite shade of green. And though most of my fantasy preferences involved darker men, he had a magnetism about him that drew the eye. I couldn't look away. His intense, snowy eyebrows fascinated me. His skin had an almost bluish tinge.

Sol wore a halo, too. Attached to both halos was a small screen jutting out at eye level. The screen showed both me and Sol the same picture of my brain. To the side of my brain image was a list of various chemicals: dopamine, serotonin, testosterone, estrogen to name just a few. We would watch as the colors of certain areas of the brain changed, and as the numbers increased or decreased on the list to the side, and observe and catalogue those changes.

It was pleasurable but tedious work.

Mathsex.

We learned a lot, though. For one, not only the genitals stimulated sexual and pleasure changes in the brain. A certain thought might do it. A touch to the lips or ear could do it. A caress to a cheek. A stroking of the toes. In some classes we experimented with reading poetry and erotica, and watched

96

our brains respond. Some people even responded to words about mechanics or physics, flowers or sunsets. We looked at how the brain responded to photographs of animals, birds, forests, a breast, a penis.

But today we were experimenting with the body again. The teacher gave us her usual speech about how humans so easily confuse mating drive with romantic drive, about how love and lust did not always equal 'in love', and that the actual chemical drug of orgasm meant different things to different people out in the real world. We were to learn to identify the differences, and be professional about it all in our own responses.

Sol began on me with a massage. I lay on my stomach and watched my monitor as he started at my head, massaging my scalp, lightly pulling his fingers through my hair.

Already my skin puckered with little shivers.

He moved to my neck and shoulders, kneading my muscles, releasing chemicals into my system. My brain lit up in different areas. I noted the levels of chemicals, very alert for this lesson at first. But as he moved over my body, I got sleepy and lazy. I could look at the recording later, and write the required essay about my feelings as the colors and numbers on the screen changed, but I was a good student and always wanted to pay attention as things were happening.

Sol's palms pressed and circled my lower back. His hands were well oiled and strong. He moved on to my buttocks, taking his time, trailing his fingers teasingly over the crack of my ass, spreading my cheeks and teasing the pucker of my anus. My brain flashed lots of red in three different areas. I felt my cock stirring beneath me. Twice he popped a slick fingertip into my hole, but then he moved on.

I sighed dramatically, squirming.

Sol said, "Charming little ass," and I watched the colors on the screen respond to his words.

He worked on my legs and ankles, my feet and toes. He took each one of my toes in his hands and massaged them. I thought I might be able to come just from that. My dopamine levels agreed. I remembered that sensation for my later essay.

"All right, turn over," he instructed.

I looked around me. Other naked students were in various states of arousal, some on their backs, some on their stomachs. Every single one of them, male and female, was getting the massage of their life from their trainers.

I gawked at one girl beside me, legs spread wide, getting an intense internal massage with her trainer's finger moving inside her in gentle, breezing motions, his other hand massaging her hairless, naked mound just above her budding scarlet clitoris. He would not touch that area on her until the session was close to over. Still, I had learned that most females, if properly aroused, could come from other kinds of stimulation. She was moaning loudly, watching her screen through slitted eyes. She might not last until he stroked her there.

I was beginning to think that was maybe the point of this lesson.

Sol stroked the fronts of my legs. His fingers delved into the muscles of my thighs with delicious grips. My balls ached. My cock leaned stiff against my belly.

He slicked my hips and all around my cock but never touched it. The tip was wet and glistening with need.

I tried to focus on the screen, on the lit up areas of my brain, green, yellow, blue and red. So much red.

Sol pressed and molded the muscles of my stomach, my diaphragm, my chest. He circled the nipples, brushing each one with oil only once. They stood up hard and ready for more touch.

He massaged my neck, my jaw, my cheeks forehead and temples.

Finally, his hand trailed down my chest, slippery and slow, until it came to my cock. He circled it.

I watched my brain colors undulate. My reptilian core for craving was all lit up and flashing red.

He picked up my cock and held it at the base so it stood straight up from my body. His thumb stroked the underside just above the balls. The tip heated with more pre-ejaculate. My brain chemistry went crazy. I tried to keep track.

His thumb kept up the rubbing. I was so hard, and I felt my organ quiver as if it grew even bigger.

Intent on the screen, I felt a moist softness touch the tip, probe the opening. I looked away from the screen and saw Sol flicking his tongue against the head of my penis, barely touching it, light, so light. His thumb stroked toward my balls. Nothing more. And the tongue tapped, moving away, coming back, flicking at the opening.

I couldn't look away. The light fell through Sol's white spiked hair, turning it silver. His green eyes glittered. And that tongue of his, moist and red, kept flicking and licking.

Everything inside me seemed to pull back, then rise forward like a tide.

I gave a tiny moan and suddenly my cock was rapidly spurting in Sol's face, jet after jet of white semen. Sol said, "Good boy." He stroked up my cock very lightly for the last spasms, catching some of my essence in his mouth.

The world spun. I got dizzy from that orgasm.

"I so love the taste of you," Sol said as he licked every drop of me from my cock, my thighs, his hands.

When I was clean, I noted on my screen the brain colors had gone from red back to mostly yellow, green and blue, and that my chemical levels slowly sank.

Sol took the halo from me and put it with his, which he set aside on the grass beside the mat. "Think about this," he told me, stroking my hip. "Essay due tomorrow."

I couldn't even consider moving. "M'kay," I mumbled.

"Do you want to sleep?" For the new boys a brief nap after orgasm was allowed. But no more than fifteen minutes.

"M'kay," I said again. "Thank you, Sol."

"You're always a pleasure, Antares," he replied.

When I woke from that dream-memory in Dusk and Nile's bed I thought: *There's an area in my brain right now that's almost filled up with red. It won't recede. In school, when a color wouldn't recede, they call it an addiction. It happens to everyone at different stages and for different reasons. But this time, Slate put it there. And now, because I want what I can't get, I have to suffer.*

Maybe, in a few months time, the craving would go away.

Chapter Thirteen

In the morning, Dusk brought me breakfast in bed but I wouldn't touch it. He put it aside and sat by me; his dark brown hand clasped mine to his chest. He kissed the top of it.

Nile stroked my hair.

"It has something to do with Slate, doesn't it?" Dusk asked.

I leaned into Dusk's shoulder and closed my eyes.

"He doesn't want to talk about it," Nile said softly. He lounged on my other side. They were both naked, as they preferred to be in their entire slave lives as well as here on the starship. Just as I had preferred until I donned the satin scarf. Dusk's skin glowed like the night. Nile, the lighter one, seemed suffused with light.

"But if Slate hurt him, shouldn't we do something?" Dusk asked.

I trusted them both. They'd been my best friends in the harem. As lovers, they had separate trainees so they'd be less distracted. That was why Dusk had never been trained by me. But Nile, sweet Nile. He had been one of my favorite trainees.

Over my head, they spoke to each other, arguing about whether to question me more or let me brood.

I interrupted them softly, "I'm in love."

They both stopped talking and looked at me.

"Did you say 'in love'?" Dusk asked.

I nodded. Finally, a few tears spilled over my cheeks. Then more. They would not stop coming. My throat was raw with them.

"With Slate?" Nile asked.

I nodded. "But he hates me."

"No one could hate you, Antares," Nile said comfortingly.

"It's true," Dusk said. "You must be mistaken."

"He told me to leave. Last night, he pushed me from the bed."

"Huh. His loss, the fool."

"Shhh!" Dusk said, lightly smacking Nile on the top of the head. "What happened?" he asked.

"Where he was raised, 'whore' is a bad word. He thinks that's what we are," I tried to explain over my stuttering breaths.

"But it's not a bad word," Nile said.

"Not to us. How do you explain our culture to someone who's never lived in it?"

Dusk said, "Well, Nile is right. He's being an idiot. It's not that hard to understand. We revere pleasure. It's natural. What's so complicated? And 'whore'? I don't even really know what that word means, actually. That you sell your skills, your art? Well, then, everybody's a whore."

"It means you let yourself be used," I said.

"Okay, but that's not how Anadans live," Nile said.

"Did you explain it like that to him?" Dusk asked.

I let out a pained laugh. "Please. He grew up on the streets of some backwater planet. He hasn't really told me in words, but I could tell from his tone, his hesitation. He only saw the seedy side of sexual manipulation and games. Maybe he was even a part of it at some time. For him, any angle he looks at it, it's seedy. Demoralizing."

"And yet he slept with you."

"Only two nights. One and a half, actually. The second night he pushed me out. We started talking and things just got rapidly out of hand. I didn't see it coming. I should have." The tears stung again. I smacked the back of my hand against my eyes angrily.

"Oh. Talking." Dusk nodded rapidly.

Nile smirked. "Totally over-rated, that talking stuff."

"Big mistake."

"Yeah. Communication sucks."

Dusk added, "Language. Humanity's biggest flaw."

"And most especially if one is in love."

Dusk nodded agreement.

Through my tears they both looked so blurry and pretty. So intent on me. Worried. Trying to be helpful even in their sweetly, sarcastic humor. I reached out and pulled them both to me. They came willingly into my arms. "Thank you, guys," I said softly.

"Anything we can do to help," Dusk murmured into my ear. "But seriously, if words don't help the situation, you need to show him how strong and smart and wonderful you."

My two dear friends stroked and consoled me all morning and afternoon. They brought me hot drinks. They dried my tears with silk. They kissed my damp, flushed cheeks.

Dusk asked me if I thought I would want to talk to Slate again.

"I don't think he'll see me," I told him.

"Then get up. Walk around. Go to the rec room. Let him see you. Show him without words. Let him see the best thing he's ever known. I dare him to resist you."

I touched Dusk's handsome face with the palm of my hand. "You're so good to me."

"Antares, you're the most beautiful of the Anadan pleasure slaves to come in a generation. And one of the smartest. You have to remember that."

There had been many farces about my supposed extraordinary beauty. In truth, there were many I'd known who were quite a bit more beautiful than I. And for those who weren't fortunate to be born with enticing features, they could buy them. Beauty enhancement was an easy, common practice.

I'd had no enhancements, though.

"You won all the beauty contest when we were in the harem together," Dusk reminded me.

"Those were beauty contests I didn't even enter." I rolled my eyes. In the harem, I had 'titles' I ignored. *"Best Natural Beauty." "Best Face." "Best eyes." "Best hair." "Best ass."* Silly games for the silly new trainees. Others came along, though, and took the titles for themselves. I never let it go to my head.

"People voted for you anyway. Write-ins. Antares, you're unforgettable. And without enhancements. But all that aside, love doesn't discriminate. Your beauty might actually make it harder on Slate. Remember our lessons? *Beauty can distract others from seeing your true core.* But if you love Slate, you have to try everything. Beauty. Brains. All of it. If he has any feelings for you, and everyone with a brain can see that he does, he won't resist you. This is just a hiccup."

"Everyone can see it?"

"Sure. His eye roams on you. Mostly when you're not looking, so maybe that's why you're so damn slow about it. But he notices you. He noticed you first of all of us in that hold when they broke through the door."

They were the best at shoring me up. Supporting me. Comforting me. Dusk and Nile. I'd always envied what they had. And when I thought we were all going to die, not ever finding love like the kind they shared had been my last, biggest regret.

Now I was afraid my biggest regret would be almost having had it and letting it slip away.

I finally agreed to their plan. I ate a meal and felt a bit stronger. I took a bath. Nile brought me scented soaps and lotions, though we Anadan pleasure slaves never needed them. But for my eyes, which were still red, they dabbed some healing lotion on the chafed skin.

Nile brushed my hair and left it down about my shoulders. It shone in the bathroom light like spun gold.

I told them Slate wanted me clothed, but I wasn't ready for the idea of being fully garbed. Dusk brought me an almost sheer flowery silk scarf for my belt. It went over my groin and between my legs and fastened in back. It was dyed lavender, pink and blue. My skin looked ultra-bronzed against those colors. Nile brought me a gold vest from one of the crew, with metal clasps, like locks, down the front. Then the chaps. They were leather and hugged my calves and thighs, while leaving the groin open so that my colorful silk scarf could still be seen in front and back. The sides of my buttocks in back were exposed. In front the chaps revealed the tops of my thighs and my hips which the scarf did not hide. The vest was high enough that my mid-drift also remained bare. Finally came the boots. At first they hurt. They were ankle boots, black with gold laces down each side. The laces matched the vest. After I walked around in them for awhile I got used to them. Nile dabbed some black stuff on my eyelashes saying it would darken them like dye.

When they were finished, the two of them looked me over and declared, "Too gorgeous for words."

For the first time, I smiled. They were two of a kind.

"Thank you both." I hugged them hard.

The evening hours approached. I had to force myself to go out of the room.

I took a computer from the storage locker and went to the main rec room on the stateroom deck. Dusk and Nile followed me, but discreetly, pretending they were not aware of me. It felt good to have their support.

I wondered if Slate had any friends on his crew. If he had talked to anyone or stayed to himself. Maybe he'd gone off to engineering again to get lost in flashing consoles or torn out bulkheads.

I sat at the table next to the corner table Slate and I used so often. I wasn't feeling so bold as to actually sit at our table right now. Then I concentrated on the screen. Of course I saw nothing but squiggles and colors. I could barely concentrate at all. But no one could tell I wasn't engrossed as I tried to look studious, alert.

I flipped through unseen pages. I tapped the screen. I pretended to type.

I found an old classic novel by Ray Bradbury and began to read.

Tonight was one of the nights Ocean came in to draw his usual crowd. He had something special planned, he said. Not just the usual fare. I didn't care, but I pretended to smile and enjoy myself anyway, keeping the computer with me for distraction.

After awhile, Ocean and two other pleasure slaves, a male and female, began to do an intricate naked dance. They wove in and around each other, a graceful, beautiful dance with teasing sexual acts meant to entice, like art—Slate's least favorite word for it, I thought, gritting my teeth—and not to show only the orgasmic outcome. They did lifts and bends and amazing acrobatic feats I had never known Ocean could accomplish so well. They made a human knot, then undid the knot, came and up and around and over each other. Here and there an erect cock would go into a mouth or ass or vulva, then come out as the movements continued to circulate, undulate. They were like a living sculpture of raw muscle and power, golden and glimmering, their hair like shining arcs of light, their muscles strong and curved, their genitalia alive and magical.

That these beautiful beings in this ornate dance could be relegated by some narrow-minded people to a status of mere "whores" mystified me. They glimmered. They surpassed their humans skins and wove a net that surged outward, encompassing all around them.

Slate finally came in. The dance continued.

I had thought he might not show. But he wasn't an anti-social sort of guy, and his crew loved him, loved having him around. It was true he did hold himself aloof at times, but his personality filled a room. He could afford to allow others take the center, express themselves.

Out the corner of my eye, I saw him approach the wine counter, but I refused to look up. Did he even glance at the dance? Could he not see the luminescence of angels that inhabited this very starship in a slide-space to nowhere?

He was an imposing shadow by the counter, his dark jeans, his vest. Hair like space. Almost an antithesis to the creatures of light that wove a tapestry of eroticism against a backdrop of stars.

My body flushed all over. I so wanted to look at him. Instead, I met Dusk's eyes in the crowd. He gave me a partial smile then made a motion with two fingers pointing at his eyes, then at me to tell me Slate had at least glanced at me.

I bowed my head tighter over the computer. My skin prickled.

Slate went to the corner and sat with his glass of wine. My whole body was aware of him. My nerves were frayed.

A couple of Slate's crew came over to him and words were exchanged. I couldn't hear them.

Ocean and his cohorts continued the dance.

The crewmembers left. Slate stayed seated for about another five minutes, then got up, leaving his glass of wine untouched on the table, and left the room.

Tears brimmed in my eyes, making me furious. I watched the colors on the computer seeing nothing.

A hand touched my head, stroked toward my neck. Nile leaned down and kissed my hair there. "Baby steps," he whispered. "Come by later. You can sleep with us again."

*

The two of them hugged me tight. Dusk and Nile. Generous, open, young and sweet. They almost seemed unaffected by everything around them, including being displaced from the only world they'd ever known. Maybe it was because they were so in love. All they needed in the entire big bad galaxy was each other.

Their bed was wide enough to hold all of us because they'd moved two regular beds together. They had somehow blocked the crack between the mattresses so where I lay was a smooth, seamless cushion.

Dusk kissed me on the lips. Nile stroked my back. An errant hand petted my cock. It did not rise.

They didn't test me further. They only politely asked permission from me if it was okay if they played with each other. Of course they had my permission. I'd seen them make love with each other dozens of times. I could no more deny such beauty than I could the stars themselves.

I moved to the side of the bed, closed my eyes and fell to sleep listening to their lovemaking, their sweet voices murmuring affections and ecstasies.

Chapter Fourteen

I dreamt again of the harem. That made three nights in a row now.

By the pool, the shadows of twilight lapped the grasses and trees surrounding us in the arboretum. Night flowers burst their pollens. The air was like wine. The lights of the pool made the waters glow sharp, almost neon blue.

At night, after the meal, we students were encouraged to play together. We were all young, virile and strong, but our enhanced libidos meant even more than usual cravings for sexual release. With that change made to our bodies, combined with a couple of fifteen minute power naps each day, and lotions to eliminate chafing, we first and second year trainees were ready for sex at a moment's notice.

About a dozen boys and girls swam naked in the pool, doing flips and somersaults, and volleying beach balls. Another dozen or so had paired off, copulating on the decks and under the trees.

I had my favorite group of boys. There was a steady line up of six of us that got together all the time. We tried all sorts of things together. It was a lot of fun.

There was a type of lounge chair made for sex that we loved to use. You could kneel on two soft arms that separated in the middle, spreading your legs and leaving a space behind you. The front had a cushioned bar where you could lean your chest, that lifted you a little, so your cock jutted forward into another open space. And your head was at the perfect position to receive. So on this chair, you could be sucked, fucked and do some sucking all at the same time.

Being young, I wanted it all. I wanted to be open. I couldn't get enough. I wanted every orifice filled. My friends were only too willing to oblige.

That night I was tireless. All the boys took turns fucking me on that apparatus, and then I took turns sucking them off as well, thirsting for their sweetness. We used up an entire bottle of oil. My own cock was never ignored. Someone was always taking care of it, stroking and sucking. I came twice without ever losing my erection.

But after the second time I came, spasming into one boy's delightfully over-friendly mouth, I realized I was dreaming because everything changed. The light in the pool suddenly went out. Now I could see everyone only in silhouette.

The boys left me. I could feel their presences still behind me, but they were silent and still. The water of the pool went quiet, as if the swimmers had all frozen place.

I heard something like a strange drumming in the distance. I strained to see. I couldn't move because the straps of the lounge that helped hold me in balance were still in place. No one had thought to undo even one of my hands.

I squinted through the dark, trying to see, my butt up in the air, my cock still half-hard, jutting out in front just below me.

The drumming was slow, methodical, like a deep heartbeat. Thump. Clump. Clomp. The sound grew louder. I still couldn't see.

Then through the darkness, far down one of the tiled paths that wound into and beyond the trees, I saw a shadow moving. I realized it was gliding forward, and the drumming, clomping sound was coming from it.

Footsteps. Heavy and laden.

I started to squirm. Whimper. "Hey, guys!" I half-whispered, my voice gruff. "Get me off this thing!"

No one responded to my plea.

110

The shadow grew. The drumming became a pounding as it moved up the path. I pulled hard at my left hand but it was fastened too tight. I tried my right. Same thing. I struggled and squirmed, trying to get my feet loose. No success.

"Guys! Help me! Guys!" My whisper rose to a harsh command. No one answered.

The shadow formed into a man. Tall and dark. Moving with a kind of fury in his gait. Only a glimmer of light shone from the stars above the arboretum ceiling, but it was enough to see. Black hair. Firm jaw tightened under the grim set of the mouth. Eyes dark as storms. He wore a white shirt and over it, a long coat with a pleated skirt that touched his knees. His heavy, leather boots had scalloped ridges along the front and back. A ridged, reptilian shape. Like a dragon's spine.

I knew him.

My hair fell in my eyes, damp from the perspiration of my fear. I struggled harder, but the straps only ate painfully into my flesh.

He came closer, those heavy boots stomping the tile. He was coming straight for me.

"Get away!" I yelled. Pulling again, feeling my flesh tear. "Get away! Leave me alone!"

But he did not listen. He came straight up to me and stopped, the skirt of his coat swirling about his legs. His dark eyes glared. My own flamed under that gaze.

"Don't touch me!" I yelled. "Help! Someone help me!"

He reached out and I flinched. My wrists were raw now. He undid one strap, and then the other. Then, wordlessly, he walked behind me and undid my ankle straps.

I climbed down from the lounge, righting myself with a little stumble, still dizzy from both the fucking and the pain of my struggle.

He stood before me, staring at me.

I backed up one step. "Go away."

He ignored my demand and reached out, grabbing my right wrist. I yanked but his grip was unrelenting. "Stop!" I pulled back but he held fast. "Don't touch me!"

"You don't belong here," he said coldly.

"Leave me alone! This is where I want to be."

"No," he said, and he gave one yank and I came abruptly forward. His hands grabbed for my upper arms. I began to struggle. "No. Get away. Get away!" I kicked, lashing out with my feet. All I hit was thick leather. He didn't even seem to notice. He held my arms without effort, pulling me closer.

"You're coming with me."

"No! I don't want to! I don't want anything to do with you!"

He said, "You don't get to say 'no'."

Tears spilled from my eyes. "I do get a voice. I do!"

"Not if I have enough money to choke that word from your vocabulary forever."

"No. It's not true. I get a say. I don't want you. I don't want you."

But it was as if he didn't hear me. He simply picked me up, threw me over his shoulder and stalked back through the trees.

I kicked some more. I tried to pull away. But he held me tight.

"Put me down. Please put me down," I pleaded.

He stopped. He lifted me to the ground and stood me on my feet. "Will you walk, then?"

I shook my head, my hair tangled in my tears, half-blinding my eyes. "I won't go with you."

"You will."

I started to cry. He came closer. I felt his arms around my back. "Don't you remember me?" he asked.

"I do. But I don't want to."

His arms tightened. "You don't have a choice."

I looked at his feet, at his huge, amazing boots. "I do have a choice. And it's not you. I want this. I want to go back."

Now he pulled me even closer. I smelled the rawness of him, the power. I rested my head against his shoulder, still crying. "I don't want to go with you."

"Yes you do."

"Why do you keep saying that?"

"Because you're mine."

My breath caught. My whole body flamed to life, as if on fire. The fire of life. The fire of creation. The fire of love, pulsing, surging, so strong the energy could power a star.

Slowly, my arms came around him. My tears melted into his coat. His head moved against me. And he repeated it in my ear. "Because you're mine."

Something touched the back of my neck. I woke suddenly, my body jerking up. Nile was sitting up beside me, the sheet around his waist. "You were whimpering," he said. "Crying in your sleep." He petted my back.

I took a deep breath. "I was back at the harem." My voice shook. Cracked.

"Oh." He looked at Dusk, still sound asleep next to him, then back at me. "Good times those were, huh?"

"Yeah."

We sat together in silence for a minute, then we both settled back into the bed to sleep.

Chapter Fifteen

Slate did not show up in the rec room for breakfast or lunch. It was disappointing, but Dusk and Nile stayed close by me for support.

And other Anadans came and went, making me feel even more supported when I saw that some of them had actually acquiesced to wear clothes now, many of them taking from my lead and attired in silk scarves, vests and other lightweight and roomy coverings no doubt gifted to them by the crew.

Finally, by mid-afternoon, I was too restless to play any more vid games or stay put. I went for a walk.

I found myself meandering into the engineering level, knowing myself to be hopelessly predictable and pathetic since the odds that Slate might be down there were obviously high.

I took my time moving down the shadow-haunted corridor, my heart skipping, my eyes hot.

I knew he was there before I saw him. I came around a small curve and into the open doorway of the far room where he sat as he had a couple days ago surrounded by pieces of equipment, tinkering with strange tools that emitted lights and beeps.

I stood in the doorway, arms across my chest and leaned my hip against the threshold frame.

He did not look up and for a moment I believed he did not see me. But then he said, "What is that get up you're wearing?"

"A gift from some friends." It was amazing that I could even speak to him, let alone so calmly. But it was as if my mind and body were waiting down the corridor a ways, the real me merely peeking around the bend.

"The others are copying you now, you know."

"We're assimilating. Ananda as we know it doesn't exist anymore. What other choice do we have even if we are to be sold, owned—whatever."

He still did not look up. But the devices he held in his hands went still. "Your friends. The ones who gave you the clothes."

"Their names are Dusk. And Nile."

"You're sleeping with them now, right?"

I inhaled. Was he going to get more wrong ideas from this? "Slate—"

He interrupted. "Just tell me."

"Sleeping. Yes. Nothing else."

He let out a humorless laugh.

And why should I have expected him to believe me? I'm an ostentatious pleasure slave. Sex for me is like breathing. A way of life. Why would he think I'd stopped doing it whenever I could?

My voice quiet, I said, "I needed to not be alone."

His breath came out in a huff.

I straightened and took a couple steps into the room. "You hurt me."

Now he looked up, his eyes hard, unflinching. "When you fell off the bed?"

I shook my head and my braid stroked my shoulders. "No. Yes. I mean my feelings."

"Oh. Well." He turned back to examine the device in his hands as if he were just seeing it for the first time. His hair, much shorter than mine but to my eyes much more beautiful, glowed. His broad shoulders were hunched.

"That's what you have to say? *Oh well*?"

"What do you want from me, Antares?" He looked up again. A flinty light edged his gaze.

I took another step closer, holding all my feelings back, though I could still taste anger, the metal of it in my mouth. "Nothing. Just, I thought—"

"You thought what?"

"That we—That what we—." I couldn't finish. The words stuck in the back of my throat, raw, strangling.

He shook his head and finally set aside his device. For long seconds he looked at me with no expression. Then with a gracefulness I didn't think he could manage in those bulky boots, he pushed himself off the floor and stood before me.

"It's your art, right?" he said. "I'll admit, it was very good. You used it enough on me."

I shook my head. Started to say 'no' but he kept talking.

"It's worked. You have me rather hooked, which was why I was trying to stay away."

"That's not—" I started to say, but my words were stopped when he grabbed me hard, brought me forward and pressed his lips against mine. I had no power to resist him. None at all. And not because I was a pleasure slave. This had nothing to do with my training, my libido, my enhanced so-called desires.

I couldn't resist because everything about him called me, drew me, snagged me. What he'd said in my dream was true. *You have no choice.* My heart wanted him and that was that.

Even if he couldn't say it himself, say those words from my dream—*you are mine*—I could say them in my own mind. I was his. Wrecked by him through and through.

I couldn't have said 'no' even if he was furious with me, even if he hated my very nature, the core that was me. I couldn't. I just couldn't—

I kissed him back. Hard.

Our bodies met. Through his tight jeans I felt the bulge of his cock against my thigh. My own rose, swaying against the silk. His hands roamed my back moving under my vest to

116

rub bare skin. I gripped his shoulders. My mouth opened to him.

He was less than gentle with me compared with the other times but I didn't care. I liked it. His hands gripped me and moved down, moving under the silk, clutching my ass.

I pushed into those hands, and pulled him closer at the shoulders but he pulled back. His hands came to my front between us at groin level and he yanked the silk scarf free, throwing it down. Out the corner of my eye I could see it float lazily to the deck like some alien creature with diaphanous wings.

Slate gave me no time to react. Roughly, he turned me and pushed me up against the bulkhead. My chest slammed against the hardness. I turned my head, avoiding knocking it into the wall as well. My cock trailed along the flat, cold surface and immediately lost some of its bounce. But I stayed still.

I heard Slate make a frustrated sound low in his throat, felt him fumble with himself. Then he was spreading me, dry, unprepared.

I didn't panic. I could take the rough stuff as well as any boy in my harem. My training made it possible. My training, my training—

I didn't know how to complete that thought. I swallowed against a thickness in my throat, tasted salt and more salt, everything inside and out of me burning as he pushed into me hard, all the way, my body working to keep up. To stay still. To accommodate.

I was open. Open. Everything was fine. I wanted him. I wanted him.

His cock dragged me forward and back, over and over into the bulkhead. I thrust back. Open, I told myself. I'm open and fine. I braced my hands against the cold wall. The bulkhead structure that encompassed us, held us only a few feet from the death of airless, icy space.

He pumped in and out. His hand came around to grip me and only then did I realize my cock was flaccid. My whole body pliant. For him. For him.

A sudden shock rumbled through him.

He started to pull back. I grabbed his hand, held it tight between me and the bulkhead. "Finish," I said, grounding back on him, moving my hips, forcing the thrusting to continue.

He let out a cry, said in a pinched voice, "Don't." But he was thrusting again, as if against his will, as if a spell had been cast and I was the witch. I knew his thoughts for me were warped, crazed. He had felt me, limp and unaroused, and thought me unwilling. Thought me unable to say 'no'. He was wrong but what could I do? I knew he hated me at this point even as he couldn't resist me. I could feel it in the way his still-clothed body pressed against me, stiff and uncompromising.

He went still inside me.

"Finish!" My voice came out harsh, teeth clenched. I undulated my hips. If I could get him to come he might be pliant enough for me to take over then, hold him, talk to him, reassure him.

"Don't," he said again, but I felt his cock stretch inside me. I felt him tense and then he spilled over with a strained cry and pushed me away and down even as he was still coming, a little white rain falling to the shiny deck.

My knees hit the floor. I groaned aloud, my breaths coming in sobs. I leaned against the bulkhead, shuddering, wheezing. My hair in my face. My eyes hot and damp. I wanted to reach out to him but I couldn't move.

I held my breath, trying to control myself. For a few seconds I heard nothing. Not a sound from him. Only the humming of the engineering level, the gentle thrumming purr.

Finally, I heard him take a deep breath. "Antares, I—" His voice died. After a count of two I heard him turn, heard the heavy sound of his footsteps receding quickly down the corridor. But no, he couldn't be running from me. That's not what I heard. Not that.

I had no time to call him back, tell him I was fine. Because really, I was fine. I was all right. Sobbing, yes. Maybe a little. But I was okay. Not a scratch. Not a blemish.

Everything was a-okay.

I looked around for my scarf. There it was. Resting like a big hothouse flower on the shining deck. Purple, blue and green. Dusted with fine glitter. I crawled over to it, picked it up. Soft. Beautiful like pre-evening, drifting skies.

With fumbling fingers I re-fastened it to my emerald belt, drew it between my legs and tucked at my back.

I stood shakily, breathing hard. Steady, I told myself. Just steady.

I had learned balance and control in the harem. How to stand tall. How to be proud of my gift.

This time it was Slate who was hurt, not me. Though maybe he didn't know that yet.

I walked slowly down the corridor, my breaths coming a little slower now, my tears drying.

The thrumming pulsed all around me, making soft entrances in to my heart.

I had the sudden thought that I wished I was drunk. I thought: My planet is on fire, the way of life I knew gone. I am on fire. Not even the breath of the stars can cool me.

Some day, I thought, *I will turn back to stardust. And everything will be at peace again, as if I had never been. Some day.*

But right now I needed a drink. Maybe two.

I headed for the rec room on the stateroom deck, and my friends. If I knew them, they were already half-drunk for the day on the ship's great stores of wine. I hoped so, at least. For their sakes.

And mine.

*

I sat on one of the couches facing the star field. I'd lost count of the glasses of wine.

Dusk and Nile tried to talk to me. They sensed my disturbance. My sweet good friends. But I said nothing except to ask for more wine, which they plied me with without question or judgment.

I kept staring at the stars, those trillions of sparks, of suns spattering the universe with their licking, probing fires. And in this galaxy alone trillions upon trillions of beings existed, breathing, living, loving, dying.

In all of that, how could it have ever come to pass that Slate and I should meet? It was beyond wondering. I couldn't even imagine how two such far-flung beings as we could ever, in the entire ancient existence of the universe, come together.

It had to be a dream. All of it.

An unreal, sleepless, aching and desperate dream.

Hours passed. Everyone went off to bed except me. Dusk and Nile tried to get me to go back to their stateroom with them, but I said no. "Maybe later," I told them.

My thoughts moved like languid flowers in a slow breeze.

I remained on the couch on my back, hands under my head, knees bent. In the mid-hours of the night you could hear the quiet hum of the starship through the deck and bulkheads, like a live thing singing along its journey.

My mind was filled with red light. Like the lights of my brain had been during mathsex, only this was far greater in magnitude. This light didn't retreat. It just kept craving. And the more I was denied my craving, the bigger that light got.

Slate had to be feeling it, too. I knew I wasn't wrong about that. What we'd shared, whether he'd admit it or not, was a kind of power that rarely comes between two people.

I couldn't stop worrying about him, what he must be feeling right now, a kind of shame that had made him run from me. But I had never denied him. I had not. But how could I tell him and have him believe me?

Was I a fool to keep pursuing him? And yet, how could I stop?

I could think only of the loneliness I saw in his eyes just before he grabbed me in the engineering. I kept remembering the way he'd clutched me, then the way he pulled back. And how I held onto him, kept encouraging him even after he thought he was raping me.

He would not see that though. That part he would forget and he would think of himself in shame. I had heard the crew talk about him over time, describing him sometimes as prudish, Victorian. He wasn't. I knew him, though, felt how he was with me. Nothing he did sexually was casual or cold. He had to be, even now, in a kind of terror over what he thought he'd done.

My mathsex teacher would simply say: it's all chemicals. She would stress that everyone faced varying degrees of these chemicals throughout their lives and for the worst one she called "romantic love" there was, quite simply, no cure at all. It was the most addictive drug in the universe once you had a taste.

Even the best-trained slave was not immune. We could learn everything there was to know about brain chemistry but still, in the end, feelings trumped logic.

The lights were dimmed for night cycle. Nearing three A.M.

I'd been lying here long enough. I had made my decision.

I got up, walked in a restless circle once about the rec room, then exited into the corridor

My legs knew where I was going even if my brain was slow to follow.

Slate did not keep his stateroom door locked. "The Captain's Quarters" were always open.

I went in without hesitation but when I got one step through the door I stopped.

I could see him in the bedroom area. He was lying fully clothed, boots off, on his rumpled bed facing away from the door. He was not asleep. I knew this because he immediately turned his head and squinted through the dimness. Very quietly, he said, "Get out."

"No."

"I don't want you here." Then he said it again. "I don't want you here."

"But I want to be here," I answered. I could see dust motes on the air in the low illumination. Through them, his tired face looked so resigned, sad. My own tears had dried hours ago, but my eyes still stung, my throat full of gravel.

"You have to stop. You have to leave me alone. After what I did I—"

"What did you do?" I interrupted.

"Don't be dense."

"I'm not. If you're referring to this afternoon, I wanted it." I dared to take a step further in, closer to the sleeping area.

"But I could tell. You didn't want it and yet I still did it."

"I *did* want it."

"You weren't aroused. You wanted to say no and I never gave you the chance."

"That's not true!"

"You were crying when I left you."

"Because I wanted more. I didn't want you to stop. I didn't want you to leave me."

"That's a lie. I saw you. I can't do this. You have to leave." His eyes were bright. Shining with emotion I'd never seen before. My chest filled with a strange, stabbing pain. He turned in the bed, his back to me. I stood by the closed door, not moving, listening to his breathing which came suddenly hard and uneven.

Maybe thirty seconds I stood there, my own tears threatening. Then slowly I reached down and took off my boots, my chaps, my vest. Clad only in the silk scarf and belt, I went to the bed and climbed up on it, lying full-length on my side and pressed up against his back. I draped my free arm over his waist.

I continued to hold him like that until his breathing evened out. He never moved. Neither of us said another word.

Sleep came like a weird and liquid light.

Chapter Sixteen

We woke early, my arm still draped across him, and he said, "You're still here."

We had had maybe three hours of sleep.

I raised myself up on my elbow and looked down at him. "Where would I go?"

He glanced away, eyelids lowered. "To your friends."

"But that isn't where I want to be."

He lay on his side, still facing away from me. "I can't even look at you. Please just leave."

"No. It's okay. I'm okay." I pushed myself closer, my hand against his shirt, my face pressed to the earthy scent of his vest twisted against his back.

"No. It's not okay!" His voice came out with a strained tone.

"It *is* okay."

"I didn't want to do what I did to you." Softer now. Exasperated.

"You did nothing to me that I didn't want." How many times would I need to say this?

A long silence followed. I measured my breathing to his. I didn't want to disrupt anything around him. I just wanted to be. With him.

His voice began to weave around me, and I realized he had started talking from a harsh, deep place in his throat, a hidden place where dark things well. His voice was liquid, fused with whispers.

"When I was fourteen—on the streets with the cold, the damp. On the streets where the tar and the oil of the blacktop got on you, into your skin and you could never wipe it clean, I—"

I heard him swallow. Inhale.

"I was raped. On those streets where I grew up. I was—
"

I lay beside him and let the story spin around and around me.

He told it in false starts. Stutters. I kept my breathing shallow, my heart open.

"My family was gone. Only a few months. I'd spent most of that time looking for passage off-world."

I wanted to know why his family had gone. Had they abandoned him? Had they died? I remained silent.

"Afterward, they kept me for a week in some apartment infested with fleas, forcing me to have sex with anyone who came to pay for it. One night one of the ropes they had tied me down with broke. I got away."

My chest moved against his back, in tandem with his own harsh breathing. My hand pressed lightly at his sternum, just under his heart against the white cotton of his shirt.

"It's very hard for me to see any kind of sex for sale that isn't something that others wouldn't manipulate for their own gain or worth."

He pulled a little away from me on the bed.

Speechless at this confession, all I could do was wait. But he was done. No more words.

The room swam in a kind of static haze. Crisp. Serene. Humming.

I felt his breath catch. Then a whisper. I almost didn't catch the words. "How could I have done that to you?"

"Passion," I said.

"You're wrong."

Softer, "Love."

"No," he said. "I don't see how that could be."

"I do." My breath brushed against his neck. "I see it very clearly."

Finally, he turned in my arms to face me. His hair fell around his face, a dark and curving shadow. His cheeks were wet. His hand came up and settled lightly against my jaw. "I'm sorry," he said. "I'm sorry about—about what I did to you..."

I pulled him against me. His wet cheek met the bare skin of my chest. "Don't." I said it over and over. "Don't."

We stayed that way for a long time.

I whispered, "You did nothing I didn't want you to do. I promise."

He exhaled hot onto my neck. The hand that had touched my jaw now gripped hard at my shoulder.

My brain was filled with red. "Do you understand?" I held him close, but I still felt separate. That I could still lose him. "Tell me you understand. Tell me you don't think I ever slept with you because it was some job for me to do. Or a game. Or that I teased you."

He started to shake his head. "To sell yourself. It's against everything I believe."

"Okay, but my self is all I have. I think I, as a being with free will, get to make that decision for myself. I'm not from your streets. I'm from a culture that revered people like me. But that's beside the point. Nothing about me, or what we are feeling here is about force, or coercion, or payment," I began.

"Shut up," he interrupted, but his voice was soft, thoughtful.

"Slate--"

"Just be quiet."

His breath warmed my skin. Where his body touched mine, I began to feel a subtle language from it, that he was really trying to feel me, who I was, what I was, so different from him, but not, our hearts agreeing more than they disagreed.

There was a moment I couldn't quite define when I sensed the release in him of some long-held idea, or belief.

126

Maybe it was in the way his weight shifted against me, or the way his eyes closed, then opened, so lazily. Or the way his gaze became so still.

After awhile I felt damp lips against my skin at my chin, at my throat. My own lips quirked but I was still too afraid to smile. Afraid I would continue to lose him. Afraid this was all a dream.

Back in the days of the harem, time was like glass, clear and clean. The future held all our worship and amazement. Every day we woke to the wonder of where we were, a heaven of pleasure upon pleasure. It was easy. We didn't have to think, though we were far from stupid. The purity in our hearts and minds pushed us into a transcendent state, a high spiritual grace.

No worries and orgasmic clarity. Paradise.

But now in a few short weeks everything had become hot and risky, terrifying and fraught with as many lows as highs. Away from my homeworld, with everything new and strange, love was messy, sex was not a universal language but instead a thing of so many different meanings, beliefs, myths.

Back home, I had been brought to sparkling orgasms by technical geniuses perfect in their stimulations. But with Slate, everything suddenly went beyond technical and into other realms. The fact that one person could do that to me was unbelievable.

Lying barely clothed beside him, I watched as Slate slowly, agonizingly came to life. He kissed my neck for some time before finally lifting his head. With his fingertips he began to explore my face. His pupils expanded as he looked at me, brown eyes wide, lashes still wet and slightly mashed, lips open just a fraction. He placed careful kisses upon my forehead, eyes, cheeks, nose, and chin.

He ran both hands down my arms. He wove his fingers with mine, petting, holding. I lay passive and watched him with fascinated wonder. He caressed my chest, my erect nipples, slowly running his fingers in lazy circles on my skin.

My body heated all over, the flush rising and stirring my cock beneath its silk covering.

He came up from my side and straddled my thighs. His hands trailed down my ribs to my waist and hips. Over my stomach, both his hands at my side now, he began to undo the buckle of my belt. He tugged it until it came lose and pulled it and the scarf entirely from my body. The emeralds flash in the dimness as he tossed it. It clunked to the floor.

My skin prickled at the loss. I was rarely without my belt, even when bathing. I still wondered if this was him placating me, keeping himself from having to listen to me try to convince him that my life was my choice, even if his wasn't.

Then he did something that let me know his mind had changed, even if only a little. Looking directly at me, he lifted his hand, the chained one with the slave bracelet on the wrist. His other hand worked at it until a fastening on the underside came loose. He wound the links over and over until they came away from his wrist.

"I always wore this so I would never forget. Like your belt, it became a part of me." He pulled the chain harder until it unwove from his fingers, then set it aside with my belt. "To me, it means I will never be owned, pinned down to a set fate. I will make my own reality."

"You should leave it on, then," I said quietly.

"Maybe I don't need it to remind me anymore."

He leaned over me, put his head down and buried it at my stomach. He kissed me there up and down, side to side. It was an action no one had ever done to me before, his lips feather-light, moist but tidy. Different. And so filled with affection.

My cock jerked. I gasped against a crack of dryness in my throat. Water filled my eyes, but it didn't sting. Not sadness or grief, but tears of pleasure. At what he was doing, yes, but more from his gesture with the bracelet, from his words.

I dared in that moment to believe I wasn't going to lose him after all.

He sucked at my hipbones, delved his tongue into the hollows beneath them. His hands moved under me as if to lift me, but he just held them there, held me, my flesh in his soft palms, and began to kiss the insides of my thighs.

I had to be dreaming, for when had I ever been made love to like this?

No one had ever made me so euphoric.

Finally, he pulled one hand up and over me, cupping my balls, his thumb gently massaging. He bent down and licked a warm, wet line up the underside of my cock.

I could not hold back a groan.

Then he left my cock and came back up to my chest. My face. He cupped my cheeks, bent and kissed my lips with a light sucking, little licks. *His* kiss. The effect of it was like being dipped in warm water as he pulled back from my mouth and returned to it over and over, his tongue finally invading, meeting mine.

My hands moved on their own, touching his sleeved arms. Gripping.

Though I'd worn my hair down the previous day, I had braided it today.

He reached over me and took the braid in his hand. With strong fingers, he broke the tie and undid the braid, tangling his fingers through it until it was loose. He put one hand behind my head and lifted it, pulling all my hair up, then combing his fingers through it above and beside my head on the pillow.

"It's like liquid running through my fingers," he murmured.

He leaned down to my face again, one hand still in my hair, and began the kissing as if starting over. I was broken open by this, hard and wanting, but soft and melting as if dripping through the sheets, the mattress, the very deck itself.

I put my arms around his shoulders. He was kissing me as deeply as he could but I wanted him closer. He trailed kisses over the side of my face and onto my left ear. His mouth nuzzled my neck again and the pleasure of that went straight through me.

I was gasping now, but he continued to take his time.

"Slate." He lifted up despite my desperate grip on his shoulders, ran a finger over my lips, hushing me. I concentrated on the next breath, and the next.

He went down to my chest, straight to the left nipple, licking, sucking, licking. I arched up, my hands moving over the leather vest at his back. He worked my nipple for a long time before moving to the right.

He kissed his way down my ribs again, to my hips, my thighs. My hands lost their grip on him by that time. His arms lifted my legs up high, then back over my head. My cock thumped against my stomach. Ass exposed in this way caused the cheeks to part and spread. He kept one arm against the backs of my thighs to keep me in place and touched me there, right over the opening, finger circling, petting, caressing. He said, "You're so goddamned beautiful!"

I wanted him in me but I didn't think he would do it so soon after what happened yesterday. All this caressing and exploring, everything making me come unglued—I knew what it was. An apology. A reaffirmation. A reverence.

In this way he showed me his craving ran as deep as my own. He was overflowing with longing. In awe.

And what I wanted was this for always. No coming and going but this forever. Him touching me, holding me. Stroking me.

With my legs still pushed up, now he grabbed for my cock, pulling it straight down between my legs where he bent and took it in one deep suck all the way into his mouth.

I yelled out loud and could not stop groaning as he moved his mouth up swirling his tongue, catching the tip with his pursed lips, then moving down in another strong suck.

I was coming before I could even warn him, so fast I had no time to even draw my breath. My cries became inhaling gasps.

He drank every drop, groaning against my spasming cock which increased the pleasure just from the vibrations of his voice.

He let my legs down and came over me, kissing me again.

Finally, he moved to the side and pulled me to him, forcing his leg between mine, cradling me in his arms.

I reached up to begin undoing his shirt but he said, "No. I just want to hold you. Like this. Right now, just like this."

I lay completely naked against his still-clothed body, my skin shining golden against his white shirt and black vest, my legs tangled with his still all in black. He held me with an arm underneath and the other over my shoulder, palm cupping the back of my neck. He kissed me over and over. He ran his hand through my hair.

I could feel his erection poking through his jeans right up against my groin. I hugged myself tightly against him.

He ran his hand from my hair and down my back, caressing my buttocks, dipping his fingers in the crack. It did not take long before I was completely aroused again.

He said to me, "I can't believe how soft your skin is. Like nothing I've felt before."

"It's permanent, too," I said softly.

"And they took all your hair from the neck down."

"Yes."

"You're too beautiful for words. I can't resist you. I can't."

"You never have to. Ever. I will always desire with my whole being to say 'yes' to you."

"I know." Softer. "You always have. I just couldn't see it until now."

I looked up at him, his face close, his eyes so dark. I kissed him deeply. His mouth opened to me.

After some more time, he allowed me to undress him. When he was fully naked, I admired him all over. The hard tanned muscles of his limbs, the pinkness of his cock so fully erect. The tattoo of flowers on his back that gleamed in its blend of colors. Our bodies came together, skin on skin. I could almost hear the skin sizzle.

His cock trailed a wetness across my hip. I couldn't have wanted him more.

I pushed him back and set about pleasuring his body much in the same way he did for me. But I rushed my way to his cock. I had to taste it. I had to wet it with my watering mouth. It was amazing to suck him. Popping that pink head between my lips in and out, making him squirm.

When I crawled up over him, he had not yet come and he looked a little confused that I had stopped. "I want you inside me," I said.

He shook his head. "No." A long pause. Then, "I want you in me."

I sat back on his thighs, his cock and mine jutting between us for attention.

"Please," he added, when I didn't respond.

It wasn't that I didn't want to do it. I wanted nothing more. Anything and everything with him. But my mind was assessing him. Demeanor and spirit. I had my suspicions of him long before he told me his story of the streets. I suspected he never allowed anyone to touch him there. Not ever since that time when he escaped his captors and never looked back.

If this was about him proving a point with me, I would not acquiesce. It just wasn't worth the risk. I touched his face. I kissed his lips.

He said, "Antares, I want you as close as you can get. Do you hear me? Do you?"

I kissed him again. "I hear you." And again.

132

He rubbed his hands down my back, over my buttocks, caressing around my hips and between my legs. He took my cock in one hand and stroked it. Then he spread his legs and lifted himself to me.

"Put it in me," he said. "Go slow so I can feel every inch."

I leaned down and whispered against his lips, "Lube first. I'm not gonna dry fuck you." I made my tone both a reprimand and a caress.

He reached over the side of his bed, fumbled a little under the edge of the mattress, and brought up a bottle of lube. I took it from him and began to oil him up.

He had slim narrow hips, a tight hard ass. I ran my slicked hands over and around and into its crevice. When I reached to slick up my own cock, he grabbed my hands, getting the oil onto them, and said, "Let me do that for you."

He sat up as I knelt beside him. He took my cock in both hands, gently pulling it through the curves of his palms over and over. He did it reverently, with total focus and a gentle affection that made my heart quicken. It felt so grand.

There was oil all over our hands, our thighs, but also in all the right places.

He leaned back at my side and spread his knees. I caught my breath at his beauty. A vulnerable but determined expression flashed across his eyes.

I crawled between his legs and with my hands on either side of his ribs leaned down to kiss him. My cock teased his. The heat between our slicked bodies flamed.

I positioned myself a little lower and teased at the slopes of his ass as he lifted himself to me.

"Sometimes it's easier if you're on your stomach."

"No," he said. Just one word. A conviction of will. An outright gesture that communicated the lowering of any remaining barriers. In the harem, we'd all learned early on that the vulnerability of eye contact could be more intimate than fucking any day.

We'd done it before this way, but only with Slate covering me. I nodded. I moved my cock between his buttocks, stroking the crease. My body loved his, my cock encased in his softness and his heat even before I'd begun to penetrate him.

When I'd used the oil on him, my fingers had slowly worked to open him, and as I moved now I could feel he was ready. I gently pushed his legs back at the knees and he allowed it, then used one hand to guide myself into him.

His eyes closed. His head leaned back into the pillow, exposing his neck. His legs came down as I slid into him and his entire body embraced me. His feet hooked into my thighs. His arms rose over my shoulders.

I leaned down to kiss his throat. My hair fell forward. He pushed up. A groan escaped his slightly parted lips. We began to move.

His eyes opened. He cupped my face in his hands. "Antares."

I smiled and kissed him. The slick fitting together of our bodies seemed too easy, the slippery motion of me moving in and out of him, his internal muscles gripping me.

I was inside him and embraced by every part of him and I never wanted him to let go. He said my name again and I lost track of everything else, who I was, where I was. Lost as the furthest unexplored star in the universe.

And yet he held me firm, tight, so only my mind could drift up and away to that alternate universe of ecstasy that is made of fire and feathers and the nectar of golden souls.

You are mine, I heard him say from my most recent dream of him.

"I'm yours," I said aloud, pushing my cock into him, my chest against his chest, my lips on his open soft mouth.

We were in perfect unison. His cock pressed against my belly. I lifted up, sorry to abandon his lips, and reached between us to take it in my hand. Taut and trembling. A burning branch. Stiff and strong as it arched in my hand, yet wet, smooth as satin.

His arms fell away, brown against the silvery sheets. His dark head pushed back, chin up. He made beautiful sounds low in his throat. His knees pressed my hips and we pushed together, apart, together in a luscious dance of passion, of love.

The pleasure between us kept building. When I thought it could go no higher, it stretched that limit and went on.

"Antares, what are you—I've never felt anything like this. I can't hold on."

He cried out. I knew my cock was stroking that special gland inside of him. He'd never felt that before? And I realized he simply had not known what a deeper touch from a man could be like if done properly, and with trust.

I increased my tempo a little, my hand gripping his cock just below the head. His entire body shuddered. His back came up, his head. He reached out for me, grabbing my shoulders. "Oh my god…"

His cock began to pulse, the milk of it spattering his chest, dripping down my fingers. I gentled my strokes to keep him in the throes of orgasm for as long as I could. My cock stroked over his inner gland and he continued to pulse and cry out. He let go of my shoulders, fell back again, his head thrashing back and forth.

I watched him come apart beneath me, the strongest, most beautiful man I'd ever known, and felt myself explode inside him in complete and utter unity with him.

My yell echoed in the room, sending the dust motes flying. I'd gone so high. The crash came so long and exquisite I thought I was floating.

When I slumped against him, my face at his neck, we were both breathing hard. My cock slipped gently from him. He moaned in protest then turned us until we were facing each other on our sides.

Our eyes met. He scowled at me. I smiled back. "Okay," I said, "maybe a little over the top but we'll get there with practice."

His eyebrows popped up. He began to laugh. I laughed with him.

"Slate, you know this—"

"Shh." He put a finger to my lips. "Don't say anything." He pulled me to him, wove his legs with mine. Our still half-hard cocks pressed. Our chests rubbed. He put his hand behind my head and kissed me on and on.

We eventually slept in the dimness of early morning. When we woke again we took a shower together, then climbed back into bed and slept some more.

*

We spent all that day in bed. There was a lot of sleeping and heavy petting. Lots of kissing. We got up only to get water or food. Then we'd come back into the bed and fool around, only to sleep again pressed tightly together.

No one came looking for us. If Nile and Dusk suspected we were together, they'd have probably gossiped a little, encouraging people to stay away from Slate's room.

By ship's afternoon, we lay naked in the bed with glasses of crimson wine. Slate said, "It's like you're a being filled with light and I can't get enough."

"Don't you know I feel the same way?" I asked.

"I didn't. Or I was just so unsure. I don't know your people. I still don't understand them. I mean physical arousal is like eating for you, I guess. Or breathing. What does that even mean?"

"For someone like me, huh?" I was not offended. I knew he wasn't sure. He was being honest.

"It's true," I told him. "Our enhanced libidos make our sex drive a natural occurrence just like anyone else's, but increased.

"How much increased?"

"More than double. Triple, maybe. Which is saying a lot in an adolescent and I was 18 when I had the treatment. It's still different from person to person, even an Anadan pleasure slave."

"So how do you know you're attracted to someone?"

"Just like you do. My emotions. My feelings. We're still human. Both of us. All of us on this ship."

"I'm sorry for my ignorance. I'm being stupid."

"No. You can ask me anything. I want you to. Nothing you say to me is stupid, Slate. Nothing. We pleasure slaves might be trained to give sex willingly, and be indiscriminate about our partners, even, but we do have preferences. And we can love. Fall in love. All that complicated messy business. We're not ignorant of that."

"Is that—is that—" He stopped, contemplating his wine.

"What's happening here?" I finished the question for him. Strangely, my face blushed hot. My eyes heated. Very softly, I said, "I want it to be. Happening, I mean."

I waited for him to say something. Anything. When he didn't, I put my wine on the bedside table and curled up next to him. I pillowed my head against his thigh, put my arms around his leg.

After a moment, his hand petted my hair, his fingers weaving through it. I heard his other hand set down his own wine glass. He leaned forward. "Come here." He pulled me up and into his arms. He kissed me and I never tired of that. Every time his lips touched mine it felt like a beginning. There was wine on his tongue. So much drunken sweetness.

I climbed over him so we were chest to chest. My legs straddled his hips. Our cocks filled, pressing together.

"I don't know if I can keep up with you," he said at last.

"You've been doing a good job of it so far," I replied. But if he was feeling chafed or worn out I had tricks up my sleeve for that. So far, though, he hadn't complained. We rubbed lazily, unhurried.

I made him turn over again so I could trace his back. His tattoo bouquet filled my eyes with soft blues, reds, pinks, golds. The vines of some of the flowers trailed all the way down to his waist, leafy and so many greens, the whole thing spilling toward his buttocks.

"Do these flowers have names?"

Languidly, he said, "Artesia, Diva of Dawn, Crying Shame."

"Crying Shame?"

"The red one." He chuckled. Continued, "Golden Gown, Attar of Autumn."

"How do you know these? What planet do they come from? Where you were born?"

"So many questions." He started to turn.

I put my palms flat on his back and held him down, rubbing gently. "Sorry." He had told me he had drawn the art. He must've known those flowers well.

I kissed each flower and every leaf. Skin like satin. My lips pressing muscle and rib.

He turned back over and pulled me to him. His cock quivered between us. My own nestled against his stomach urging me to thrust.

It wasn't long before we were feasting on each other again.

His salt covered my lips.

Chapter Seventeen

Ship's evening had already arrived when we finally emerged from Slate's stateroom. We got ourselves real, hot meals and ended up in the main rec room.

The stars glowed on the far wall-monitor.

About a dozen crew and Anadans were there but our table was left free as if by some unspoken arrangement.

We took our usual spot. Slate poured the wine. We had steak and potatoes, green beans (not fresh but still good) and hot rolls with melting butter. We both ate like starved men.

Nile and Dusk came over to say hello.

Nile leaned down and whispered in my ear, "We're both very happy for you right now."

I answered with a smile.

Nile straightened. They stood side by side facing us.

"We think we've found the owner we want. We both have agreed. We haven't written him of our decision yet," Dusk said.

Nile added, "We've been communicating for over a week. If he passes our physical check, he'll be the one."

I had not allowed myself to focus on buyers. Not for myself, at least. And I paid no attention these past weeks to what the others were doing. I knew I would eventually say more good-byes to old friends, but it still hurt.

I would miss them.

I looked up into Nile's sweet eyes, my own blurring. "You'll be leaving?"

Nile touched my shoulder. "Silly. He knows Slate. You can visit."

But he assumed I'd be in any position to do so. Slate had not yet made a verbal commitment to me. Nor I to him.

"He calls himself Owl but his real name is Burt. I wouldn't say he's a friend but I have vouched for him in the past," Slate said.

"He's very wealthy," Nile said.

"And he really wants us as a pair," Dusk added.

I stared at my plate. Most of my food was gone, which was good because I wasn't hungry anymore.

I was happy for my friends. Truly. But all this change was still so abrupt, so hard. And still ongoing.

After our meal, Slate and I played a couple of board games. I lost badly at every turn. We watched some vids and drank more wine.

When I left to visit the bathroom I ran into Nile in the corridor outside. He said, "Antares, you two look wonderful together."

"Thanks."

"So I guess you guys figured some things out."

"It's ongoing."

"Don't worry. Everyone can see you two are in love. It'll all work out."

"I hope so."

He reached out and stroked my hair. "It will."

"I don't want to go back, Nile. To what we were. I don't want an owner. Not anymore. I thought I did. Before Slate it was all I longed for. But now—"

He grinned at me. "With Slate and his crew, no one is going to make you do anything you don't want to."

"Yeah, but if he doesn't keep me, where will I go?"

"You told me whenever I would complain, back when you were my trainer and I would cry in your arms, 'Don't worry so much, little boy. The future is not even here yet. We face it when it comes.' Do you remember that?"

I said, "I really said something that smart, huh?"

"You did."

"Well, you were a good student."

"Things are different for me, though. I've had Dusk by my side all along. And we loved our owner, being part of a threesome. We crave it again. Neither of us has to face anything alone. We want what we want together. As a team. This is what will make us happy. You have your own path and your own decisions to make. And I know it will work out for you. I just know."

"Thank you, Nile."

We hugged and I went back to the rec room and Slate.

When we were sufficiently tired again, we went back to his stateroom.

We spent the night much like the one before it. More than content in each other's arms.

*

We woke in the night again and began our stroking and kissing. He was irresistible to me and in my every waking moment I could think of nothing else.

He pushed me onto my back and hovered over me. His eyes reflected a dark brightness. His hair hung loose around his head. He said, "Do you envy Dusk and Nile?"

"You mean what they have with each other?"

"That they are going to a real home. A wealthy home. To be what their natures demand they be."

"Yes, they will be good and pampered princes again."

Slate flinched strangely at my words. "Is it what you want, too? Do you have prospects?" His voice held a subtle quaver.

"No is my answer to both questions."

"Then what have you been doing at the computer all this time?"

"Nothing."

"Nothing?"

I made a face. "Looking busy. Playing solitaire."

"But I don't understand." Now he sat up, knees bent, and hugged his calves.

"When the Empire came, everything changed. Not just outside and all the life I'd known. But inside me, too. Everything's still changing. I feel like things are moving too fast. I'm always confused. And I don't want what the others want anymore."

"That makes sense. I've had changes in my own life like that. No matter where you come from or who you are abrupt shocks to the system can alter who you are forever."

"So you know what it's like?" I wanted to ask him so many questions. Know everything. But I told myself to go slow. He was so private about his past.

"Yes. It's just that you've spent your life training and longing to be owned. It's a comfort. A desire. A necessity, even. I don't want to stand in the way of that for you."

I put my hand on his back, on the cascading flowers that permanently marked him. I took a deep breath. My heart filled up my chest. The words I wanted to say tried to stop in my throat. There were still so many blocks there, so much raw emotion. But I forced them out. Love is risky like that. Love is a gamble and sometimes the dice flies right off the table. "You aren't blocking my path, Slate. You *are* my path."

He turned and pulled me to him. We both sank back down to the bed. "I want you. I want you all the time."

"Me, too," I whispered.

His breath washed over me, tart wine, and the metallic salty essence of him I so loved. "But how do I know you won't leave me?"

My chest fluttered at such a vulnerable question. "I won't."

"How do I know you won't break my heart?"

I bowed my head. I gave him a sheepish smile. "You can't. None of us can ever know anything like that for sure. Because we're human. And because love is messy."

"And confusing," he added.

"And the biggest leap. With no guarantees."

He held out his hand to me, facing up. "Will you take that leap with me?"

"Yes." I put my hand in his. Yes. Yes. And yes.

Chapter Eighteen

I sat in the middle of his bed, turning the thing over and over in my hand.

"What is it?" I asked.

"It's a book," Slate said.

The cover was clear, like glass.

Slate said, "It's made of ice."

"What?"

"The ice is preserved by a stasis field on the front and back of each cover. The pages are made of powdered quartz, among other things."

My hands roamed the cover. I could feel tiny vibrations. It was cool to the touch but not freezing.

"It's amazing. I've never seen anything like it."

"It's very rare. From the planet Winter. Worth a fortune."

I raised it up to hand it back to him.

"No. It's yours. I'm giving it to you."

"But the cost. You said—"

He knelt at the foot of the bed and placed his hands over mine as they held the book. "It cost me nothing. I stole it. And now I'm giving it to you."

I looked down at it sparkling, not too heavy but so rich in the feel of it. "I don't know what to say."

Slate shrugged. "A 'thank you' would be just fine."

"Thank you."

"You told me maybe there was a great poet in you that you had not yet discovered. Well, use this to discover. Write your thoughts. Whatever you want. It's yours now."

It was on that day that I began to write the words that had all caught up in my throat, threatening to choke me ever since the Empire came.

I began to write my story.

And now it is almost to its end.

Months have passed since Slate and I made our promises to each other. Our commitment.

In that time I've said good-bye to old friends. Nile and Dusk write me often, happy and healthy with their new owner who loves them.

I have joined Slate's crew. When he asked me to stay with him, I knew it would happen. I knew nothing about being a thief, but in this perilous galaxy, I had no morals against it.

Being with Slate now, I've never known such a wholeness, such wonder. I'm filled up with pleasure, with a burning longing, an endless inner astonishment. I am full of impressions, ideas. Full of affection, sensation, a spirit of daring. How could I say no to his way of life? To an adventure I've always secretly wanted?

We've decided to keep the starship, hidden in slide-space, and it is our base of operations.

The core of our love grows stronger every day. We have missions together. We play together. We laugh together. And we make love.

In that, my story could not be more complete.

But there was still the question of Slate. His origins. And my curiosity never waned.

One day Slate came to me and said, "I want to take you on a trip. Just a side trip. No big deal. Will you come with me?"

"Of course. Where are we going?"

"It's a surprise."

*

We took the starship's shuttle, went into the slide, and hours later landed on a planet Slate called Lyrafel. It was night, but the lights of the shuttle hit a field of flowers and lit them up into a rainbow cascade as we landed in the middle of it.

I'd seen those flowers before. They were all over Slate's back in a beautiful tattoo.

He opened the shuttle door and the ramp came out. We walked down it and into a sugar-scented night. All around us the sky shimmered with stars. On the horizon rose a hill. Silhouetted against the stars stood a massive structure with steeples and turrets and jagged walls stretching far into the night. But even from here, I could see portions of it had crumbled away.

"This is where you wanted to take me? Why?"

"My homeworld."

My mouth dropped open.

"I used to live here."

"What happened?"

"The Empire came. They took everything, mined all the resources, leaving nothing behind for those who managed to survive."

"This field. These flowers. It's beautiful."

"They're all that's left. Weeds, actually. Beautiful, astonishing weeds."

"Did you live in a city?"

"No." He pointed to the horizon. The castle hunched into its own skeleton. "There."

"That castle was your house? You were royalty?"

"The eldest male. The anointed prince. I was 14 when the Empire came."

I could only stare.

"All this time. A prince," I said softly.

"A thief," he corrected. "That boy prince, so pampered, who thought he was so special, is dead. So you see. I do

146

understand you. I always understood. Your grief. From the first day I found you in that hold. Your loss. It is also mine."

A dead planet. A dead prince. A never-would-be king.

I leaned into him, staring at the far-off castle ruin. I reached across him. His hand came into mine.

"Thank you for bringing me here."

"Thank you for being the person this terrible life finally led to."

I put my arms around him as a cool breeze scented with iron and ash brushed up and over us. The flowers bloomed around us. They gave off a sweet scent of hope, of renewal. Some day their love for the dead planet would cover it again.

Some day.

Dear Reader:

Thank you for reading my story. I appreciate all my readers perhaps more than they can ever know.

As a poet, all my stories in all the genres I've tackled in my writing life are inspired by something poetic in nature, a painting, a word, a song, a phrase. Often, I will write a poem and it becomes a story.

"Scoundrel" became a flicker in my eye, still unborn, unformed, after I wrote a poem called "The Survivor." I'd like to share it with you here.

The Survivor

doomed princeling
your body is like a wind-bent shadow
the landscape is all lanterns
turning with the stars
you forget your name
whenever you are touched
your realm died with the last of the silver moons
the broken scepters of dead worlds
float forever
in the void-poems you recite
from this alien city's bleakest corner

As always, you can find me on my blog here: http://wendyrathbone.blogspot.com/
My Facebook page: https://www.facebook.com/wendy.rathbone.3
My author page on Amazon.com contains a list of all my books as well.
http://www.amazon.com/Wendy-Rathbone/e/B00B0O9BMS/ref=sr_tc_2_0?qid=1435096235&sr=1-2-ent
In greatest appreciation,
Wendy Rathbone

LETTERS TO AN ANDROID
Wendy Rathbone

Cobalt is a created human, vat grown and born adult, with no human rights and indentured to serve others for the duration of his life. Liyan is a young man with wanderlust in his eyes, embarking on a career that takes him to the furthest regions of space. The two become unlikely friends and create a memorable long-distance correspondence. Through Liyan, Cobalt gets to explore the universe, living vicariously through his friend's wave transmissions. A strong bond develops between them that not even the stars can put asunder.

Now you know an android who writes poetry.

This is all your fault. Did you not read my last wave telling you extracurricular activities for my kind are discouraged? Of course this is harmless and strangely enjoyable and does not necessarily require me to leave the hotel. Pel would not care if I wrote lines of equations or nonsensical juxtaposed words. As long as the act does not bring my mental state into question.

However, in history, poetry is often written by the rebels.

So we can keep this to ourselves.

Let me know about your lieutenant's test.

And to give you peace of mind, I never believed you observed me as anything other than human.

Some people are and always will be hateful bigots. Most people are simply uncomfortable in speaking to "property." And anyway, friendship, like poetry, is also discouraged.

Your friend,
Cobalt

FROM THE AUTHOR:
www.eyescrypublications.com

ON AMAZON:
http://www.amazon.com/Letters-Android-Wendy-Rathbone/dp/0989693872/

PALE ZENITH
Wendy Rathbone
A Science Fiction Novel

On a far-flung "Earth" in a parallel universe, two factions are fighting a decades-long psychic war. Young talented psychics are being temporarily kidnapped from present day Earth, seemingly at random, to serve as part of one side's psychic army. They are put under the control of spychiatrists, mysterious machines with many limbs that have a programmed ability to travel time and space and universes to kidnap and control carefully selected humans. The humans never know they are being used; when their missions are completed they are brought back to their universe through time and placed back in their beds, their memories wiped.

The shadows wound the tall corridor in muted gold, varnished brown. It seemed as though they were in the bowels of a giant serpent coiled outside time, outside space.

When they left the palace, a familiar sun flourished in a clear, blue sky. But this wasn't their sun. Not Zack's sun. It was an alien star burning within a different galaxy in an all too distant universe. Zack looked up squinting, trying to see if he could peer beyond the sky, beyond the pale of midday and into his own timespace, but there was nothing. Only sunlight. Only the thin atmosphere of an Earth not his own.

His back knotted again. Leo's presence was a gelid space inside his chest, empty. Always before he'd felt a warmth there, a sort of pressure like someone's hand pressed gently to his heart. He'd taken Leo for granted knowing, the way a shadow falls when you block the sun, that he was there around him, inside him: blood, air, salt, brain, soul. They were genetic duplicates, twins, spiritual halves. Without him, Zack knew the first icy tugs of panic.

FROM THE AUTHOR
www.eyescrypublications.com
ON AMAZON
http://www.amazon.com/Pale-Zenith-Wendy-Rathbone/dp/0976689790/

WENDY
RATHBONE

Moltenrose

Stories set in
the PALE ZENITH universe

Moltenrose
Stories Set in the *Pale Zenith* Universe
by *Wendy Rathbone*

In a post-holocaust world, a young woman and her robot partner leave their nomadic gang to take a long trek on foot to the city of Moltenrose to seek their fortune. **Green Forever** is a coming of age novella about love, death and making your own luck.

In the story **Moltenrose**, a deformed man whose nickname is 'Ugly' lives in the shadowed ruins of the barely-alive city and works in a sideshow at the tourist-trap carnival at the edge of town. His story involves several 'firsts' including a lesson about beauty.

Excerpt: "You're late, boy," Rycoff mutters as I walk under the awning and into the tent. His belly hangs over an expensive gold belt, the vinyl trousers like a plastic sack he'd forced his flesh into. He wears a fashionable long-sleeved, bulky paper shirt. White. It sticks to his arms and back. There's already a little tear in it at the wrist. He goes through a dozen a day.

"How can I be? There's no line yet."

"I pay you by the hour, Ugly. Try to remember." He shuffles by me, leaving a scent-trail of sweat and mint. The black skin of his face glistens. The white braid that flaps over his shoulder is as artificial as my half-wig. A stranger might take him for a clown, but he's as shrewd a business-person as Colere the trans-hop queen, who owns half the Free World. Rycoff's just had a little less luck.

I take Main Street to work every day. It needs mending, as does the entire city of Moltenrose. Ghost City, people call it. A fitting place for me since I'm just one more broken down part of it. And the carnival on the east side where tourism keeps what's left of it alive is as good a place as any to work.

On Amazon: http://www.amazon.com/Moltenrose-Stories-Pale-Zenith-Universe/dp/1942415001/

Our Site: http://www.eyescrypublications.com

The Foundling
by Wendy Rathbone

Diego is a powerful man with a tragic past. Out on the expansive ocean in his private yacht, he discovers a beautiful and mysterious man adrift on a raft, near death. The bond that forms between them in the aftermath of Alec's rescue is one of fierce passion, though lacking in trust. Can they make it work, or will Alec's amnesia bring forth secrets so disturbing as to tear them apart? A passionately erotic love story of desire and darkness, exquisite and explicit.

––––––––––––––

I can see his struggle between gratitude and uneasiness. He is buffeted by all things new and strange. He does not know where he is from, who he is or what happened to him. He does not know me. There has not been enough time to transition between strangers and friendship.

This isolation of his is something I can identify with, but it is also a feeling no one can help him with until or unless he gets his own life back. And his memory.

If that doesn't happen, then it will take time for him to build a new life. He is polite to me, even friendly, but even a night together during a storm with his arms wrapped tight around my waist doesn't calm the surge I see inside him, the emptiness, the loss, possibly even panic. That night may have reinforced some trust in me, but so far not enough for him to completely relax.

He seeks me out, though. That's something. He sits by me at dinner when he can have any seat of his choosing. I watch him closely when he does not realize it. At dinner the following night after we had only 'slept' together, and before we go to bed again in separate rooms, I notice everything about him, how he moves, the way the air warms when he is closer to me, the dry sheen of his lips as they part for more air when he is reacting to something, or speaking, or eating.

His hands still shake. Anyone else might not notice because he keeps them clasped into fists at his sides or, while sitting, pressed tight to his lap.

I spend another fretful night alone. I dream restlessly, wild, loud and colorful visions I cannot recall at all as soon as my eyes open. All I know is the dreams leave me unfulfilled, impatient.

www.eyescry.com/html/publications.htm

None Can Hold the Dark
Wendy Rathbone

In the eagerly-awaited sequel to Wendy Rathbone's homoerotic romance **"The Foundling,"** Diego and Alec meet new challenges in private and from the outside world. Diego is being investigated by the local police for murder. Meanwhile, Alec's amnesia and the trauma of his kidnapping by white slavers continue to plague him. And the danger to Alec is not yet over.

Distracted by their new love, both men fail to see certain threats until it is almost too late.

"Why do you keep doing this illegal business?" Now Alec's gaze turned toward him, open as the day and lit with a sad frenzy, a challenge. "You could go anywhere, do anything, be anyone."

Diego had asked himself that question on rare occasions. In truth, he got used to what he was, what he did. Even a dangerous known was perhaps preferable to the unknown. "People depend on me."

Alec shook his head, but smiled a little as he said, "That's so weak." He leaned forward, over the arm of the chair, and put his shaking hand on the back of Diego's head. The kiss was cool, lingering, moist with salt. When Alec pulled back, he said almost matter of factly, "It's like there's sharks and there's goldfish and one can't decide to become the other."

Diego was still stunned by the kiss. But the words hit him hard. In them was the unfair conjecture of a locked fate. He believed in making his own fate...or luck. Did Alec think only one kind of man lived inside him and that was all there was to it? To life? It hurt. Badly.

Diego sat back on his heels, catching himself with his hands on the smooth floor. "So, Alec, which am I?"

Alec frowned.

Diego said, "I made choices in my life. I made them No one made them for me. If I need to be strong I'm strong. If I need to be vicious I can be that too. So what? I'm stuck there? In a pattern, a role...with no free will?"

Alec watched him inquisitively now.

"Because," Diego went on, "I'm solely responsible for my actions. Me. Could you say the same of the shark?"

They both waited, the silence covering them in muggy discomfort.

"You think you understand me?" Diego finally asked.

www.eyescrypublications.com

153

The Lostling: Alec's Story
Book Three in The Foundling Trilogy
by *Wendy Rathbone*

The Lostling takes place directly after *None Can Hold the Dark*, as Alec and Diego relocate to San Francisco. There, amid salty winter wind and fog, Alec's lost memories slowly return and he must relive some of his most painful and terrifying moments to regain his forgotten self. In agonizing dreams and flashes of memory, he finally remembers what happened to him... and why.

Excerpt: *Putting a hand on his arm or leg, I can always feel the tremor of Diego even through his clothes, an innate wildness, a life-power.*

I always believed, from the first day Diego found me unconscious and dying, floating in the middle of a sapphire Caribbean ocean, there was a core of me unhidden, unforgotten, that cried out silently to the air and everything around me communicating who I am, what I am.

I can't remember it myself. Not that core, not anything up to the day I awoke in Diego's bed, sick and panicked. In that moment, I remembered nothing more than my first name, and even that memory is suspect. But this core of me demands to take things into its own hands to be seen, to make sure it remains "I am."

I believe Diego saw it, the urgent desperation in me wanting to be witnessed, and he made a promise to that essence of me, to that heart of me, that he would see me through anything that came my way. Something in me reached up and latched onto him, a clasping energy, and Diego clasped back.

It caught and held him. He was moved. He was compelled. He was mesmerized.

www.eyescrypublications.com

http://www.amazon.com/Lostling-Alecs-Story-Foundling-Book-ebook/dp/B00RO8GSUW/

My House Is Full of Whispers
Wendy Rathbone

Ten erotica short stories by Wendy Rathbone - former winner of the prestigious WRITERS OF THE FUTURE contest!

Leda has not one beautiful man, but two. Kale enters a secret world in a wealthy man's basement. Noah is in love with a man who hates sex. Dina lives next door to a famous Hollywood director she secretly loves. Dorian has a sixteen year old female student coming onto him. Tara is haunted by an erotic ghost. Young Dimitri is kidnapped by lecherous men. And more.

Author's Preface

When I wrote these stories, I deliberately set out to gently break down certain barriers, and I've certainly broken taboos. Do I care? No. This is fantasy at its purest level. The stories are never meant to be political statements, nor do they make any attempt at political correctness, and there is little consideration for safe sex. While I definitely condone safe sex, my stories come from fictional realities in my head where safe sex is not much of a concern because, well, it's imaginary and it's fiction!

For me, these stories are meant as little poetic erotic ramblings merely to stir the flames of desire, nothing more. They are pure fantasy and therefore to be enjoyed as such. Every story is erotic in nature, meant to titillate, some more explicit than others. Some of the stories are light, some are darker. I invite the reader to a feast of diversity and delight.

One reader commented: *"...some of the most beautifully written erotica since Anais Nin!"*

FROM THE AUTHOR:
www.eyescrypublications.com
ON AMAZON:
http://www.amazon.com/House-Full-Whispers-Wendy-Rathbone-ebook/dp/B00IJK3G04/

UNEARTHLY
by Wendy Rathbone

A Collection of
Award-Winning Poetry

Intro by the Author: This book contains all my out of print chapbooks (mini-collections of an author's work usually published by smaller presses.)

The chapbooks published within include:
Moon Canoes, published by Dark Regions Press, 1994
(Im)mortal, published by Shadowfire Press, 1996
Scrying The River Styx, published by Anamnesis Press, 1999
Autumn Phantoms, published by Flesh and Blood Press, 2000
Dreams of Decadence Presents: Wendy Rathbone, published by DNA Publications 2002
Dancing in the Haunted Woodlands, published by Yellow Bat Review, 2003
Vampyria, published by Eye Scry Publications, 2005

She Sleeps With Vampires
She sleeps with vampires
courting velvet breaths
poem-dreams
chill-stopped hearts

Wrapped in her arms
like teddy bear thoughts
purple lips trembling
at her quiet throat
they love her more than
somber rain
more than autumn
more than ash-soft hearths of night.

FROM THE AUTHOR
www.eyescrypublications.com
ON AMAZON
http://www.amazon.com/Unearthly-Wendy-Rathbone-ebook/dp/B00B0MTIZK/

Other fiction titles from Eye Scry Publications...

Prince of Umberlight
Alexis Fegan Black

"If Prince of Umberlight doesn't rattle your cage, you're more dead than the undead!" **-Night Readers**

Thorn may be an 800 year old vampire, but he does not possess the ability to create others of his kind, and so he is cursed to fall in love with mortals, only to watch them grow old and die. Torn by grief, Thorn denounces his immortality and enters into a comatose oblivion for decades. When he awakens, he is no longer in London, but finds himself in a world spun into being by his own desires - a world where Time and Death do not exist, a world where it is forever autumn, where the Parish of Shadows and the River of Stars become his home. It is in this world of Umberlight that he meets Atom - an interloper into his private sanctuary, but also an impudent imp who is destined to reveal to Thorn the three dangerous elements a vampire must possess in order to become a Creator.

The Art of Brutality.
Submission to Dark Desire.
Love.

FROM THE AUTHOR
www.eyescrypublications.com

ON AMAZON
http://www.amazon.com/Prince-Umberlight-Tales-Book-ebook/dp/B00TRD2EHS/ref=asap_bc?ie=UTF8

NO FORWARDING ADDRESS
Della Van Hise

When Terrans came to sail dark seas,
And see what stars might be...
Heaven moved with no forwarding
address,
And left this void to me.
(Children's song from Lazali)

A literary science fiction novel told in the voice of an empath, *No Forwarding Address* explores the lures and the dangers of love, the tragedies and triumphs stirring in the human heart.

When Crystal and Raine first meet, it is 50 years after The Great War on Earth. They are hesitant to trust, afraid to love. But even if they are able to overcome these seemingly insurmountable obstacles, is even love enough?

When a man has the stars in his eyes, legend says he must serve them above all others.

I knew then that it wasn't love and hate who were mirror twins. The final irony was that grief would always turn out to be the paradoxical antithesis and simultaneous manifestation of whatever it is that humans call love.

Crystal remained silent and walked a few steps away from Raine – further down the shoreline, until she stood under the wing of one fallen Phantom. She thought of the ship she had seen from the balcony of our home, and though it had long since disappeared over the dark and treacherous abyss of the ocean, its image lingered clearly in her thoughts. On that ship was a man, she thought. A terribly lonely man who made no great difference to the flow of time or the memory of the galaxy. A man who, like Raine, was compelled to keep moving and look only ahead and never behind. A man who could not afford the luxury of waving goodbye to friends on shore.

At last, she turned toward her beloved and watched him watching the darkness. He stood only a few feet away, yet the images in my mind said he might as well have been a million light years off in the void. He was lost to her in that instant out-of-time, just as lost and impossible to find as the light from that ship which had vanished over the horizon...

www.eyescrypublications.com
http://www.amazon.com/Forwarding-Address-Della-Van-Hise-ebook/dp/B00PEOSKJ0/

COYOTE
Della Van Hise

*A Novel of Love, Honor
and Personal Sacrifice...*

When River Willows is accused of a murder she didn't commit, her life takes a turn toward the sanctuary of a world existing at right-angles to our own. Combining the mysticism of martial arts and the romantic conflict of a young woman torn between two powerful men, COYOTE takes the reader on an epic journey of dangerous secrets, military cover-ups, and the infinite heart of the peaceful warrior.

———————

"So who's Coyote?" I asked, trying to ignore the effect he was having on me. "You?"

Steale laughed easily, though it did little to hide the torment behind that mask of indifference he wore so well.

"Coyote's a scavenger, Jack of all trades. The Native Americans call him the trickster - the one who brought chaos down on the world." He shrugged as if altogether unconcerned. "Original sin."

"Is that what you are?" I asked, keeping it light despite the growing knot my stomach. "Original sin?"

He kept his profile to me, eyes straight ahead as he drove. "Sure you want to know?"

I couldn't help wondering if I had cornered the coyote, or if the clever trickster had cornered me.

———————

By the author of **KILLING TIME** – without a doubt the most controversial **STAR TREK** novel ever published!

From the author:
www.eyescrypublications.com

On Amazon
http://www.amazon.com/Coyote-Della-Van-Hise/dp/0976689782/

YEAR OF THE RAM
Della Van Hise

Year of the Ram was described by one reviewer as... "A spacefaring gay romance full of love, angst, and longing."

Only after Star Commander Morgan Diego becomes an exile as a result of a Galaxy Corps political blunder does he begin to realize how much he valued the companionship of his second in command - the mysterious Lucien, an Alfarian who is more elven than human, with peculiar powers & abilities which begin to unfold as he, too, realizes what he has lost.

Separated by circumstance from his former life, Morgan is thrust into a world where he must survive by his wits. When he meets a peculiar little old man calling himself Kim Le, Morgan finds himself in a situation where he is required to master The Art - not only a form of human & extraterrestrial martial arts, but a way of living and being that will alter his life forever.

At the temple, he is introduced to his new teacher, another Alfarian who begins to steal his heart - a heart which is already promised to Lucien. Torn and conflicted, Morgan struggles with the world he left behind and the world he now inhabits.

Beginning to believe he may never again return to his ship and to the friends and loved ones he left behind, he is all the more frustrated and heartbroken when a new Master arrives at the temple: a man to whom Morgan is immediately drawn both mentally and physically, a man who is strikingly familiar... yet utterly alien.

Year of the Ram is a fully-fleshed novel, approximately 97000 words, with a focus on the love story and romance angle. Set against a science fiction milieu, it explores the infinite possibilities of the human and alien heart. Sexual content is explicit, though is not the primary focus of the novel.

For those who like a romance that forces its characters to contemplate the ecstasies AND the agonies of love... you will enjoy *Year of the Ram* immensely.

FROM THE AUTHOR:
www.eyescrypublications.com
ON AMAZON:
http://www.amazon.com/Year-Ram-Della-Van-Hise/dp/0989693813/

Non-fiction titles from Eye Scry Publications...

TEACHINGS OF THE IMMORTALS
by Mikal Nyght

So... You Want To Live Forever?
The teachings are presented as brief vignettes in no particular order of importance. This is not a book you read from start to finish in a single night. It is a grimoire of self-creation, intended to be contemplated slowly so as to be assimilated wholly. Pick it up and turn to a page at random. Where your eyes come to rest on the page is your lesson for the day. Go no further until you have assimilated the lesson totally.

The teachings are seduction as much as instruction. This is the way of The Dark Evolution.

The Ruby Slippers

The danger of the consensual continuum is that its natural gravity exists at the lowest common denominator of human experience, and because of this it will automatically make you forget those elusive truths you've fought to learn, and before you know it you're lost in petty dramas again, sinking into the mire of old familiar scripts.

The only way to overcome this is to be continually cavorting with worlds and events beyond human experience, journeying into the unknown so that it can become known, expanding knowledge and awareness to become more than you were, bringing back from the Dreaming those secrets which will teach you how to use the ruby slippers to transport yourself over the rainbow to the vampyre wizard's secret lair.

Perception

This is the nature of reality: to be precisely what perception dictates, as solid and whole as your interpretation of it, or as changeable and eternal as you permit it to be.

It wasn't knowledge god tried to keep from Man, you see. It was perception, for perception alone has the power to destroy god and obliterate comfortable consensual realities to create unending immortality.

Take the apple, my embryonic children. Nibble its red red flesh. Open your vampyre eyes so you may finally begin to *See*.

www.immortalis-animus.com
www.eyescrypublications.com

http://www.amazon.com/Teachings-Immortals-Mikal-Nyght-ebook/dp/B00C2HY5WS/

Quantum Shaman:
Diary of a Nagual Woman
Della Van Hise\

"Diary of a Nagual Woman brings a quantum understanding to what has traditionally been believed to be a mystical path alone. This book picks up where Carlos Castaneda left off to take us on a roller coaster ride of our own forgotten power..." - Michael Grove, Reviewer

When I asked how Orlando had known I would come to this remote location, and how he himself had gotten there – since there were no other cars in the tiny parking lot – he only smiled a little, stretched out his long legs, and slouched down on that cold metal bench to stare up at the stars.

"You're predictable," he said as if I should have already known. "I'm here because this is where you always come when you're mad at the world."

I attempted to engage him in a conversation of just exactly how he knew I was mad at the world, since I'd had no direct contact with him in quite some time, nothing to give him any hint of what was going on in my everyday life. But even as I began spelling all of that out to him, he brushed my words aside with an easy gesture.

"Do you want to talk or do you want to waste time looking for logical explanations for every magical thing that ever happens?" he asked. "That's what's wrong with the world, you know. Instead of embracing the mysteries and trying to determine how they might open a crack in an otherwise humdrum, pre-programmed existence, people waste their entire lives explaining it all away, attaching labels to it, filing and categorizing it until it loses any meaning."

He had a point. And I'd already been inundated with enough mysteries to know that some things simply had no explanation humans could understand. *'Magic is only science not yet understood'.* Words Orlando had written more than a year before rattled through my mind up there in the middle of the night, in the middle of nowhere, looking down on a distant world that seemed far more unreal to me at that moment than the world he had been trying to teach me to *see*.

He was there – whether physically or in some spirit-form is ultimately of no importance, for in the sorcerer's world there is no difference between body and spirit, and in any world, perception is reality.

www.quantumshaman.com
www.eyescrypublications.com

Scrawls on the Walls of the Soul
Della Van Hise

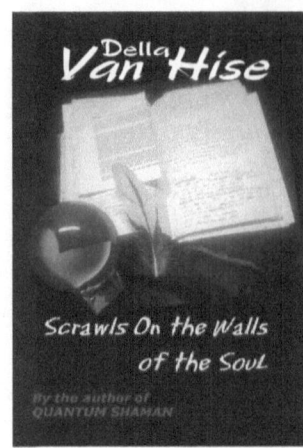

The long-awaited follow-up to
Quantum Shaman: Diary of a Nagual Woman.
Stands alone, or order together!

"If you've ever felt like a stranger in a strange land, this book is your road map to survival in the spiritual wilderness!" (Michael Grove)

~

It was May of 2000 when my mentor threw me out of the quantum cosmic classroom and said, "I've taught you everything I can. Now it's time to take that knowledge and slam it up against the walls of the real world. If it remains intact and survives the brutality to which it will be subjected, you will get a gold star next to your name and be allowed to proceed to the next level." No mention was made of what this next level might be, or if, indeed, it truly existed.

Go ahead – try to explain this all-consuming path to your friends and relatives. They will smile politely, squirm uncomfortably, and eventually they will stop returning your phone calls and look the other way when they see you coming. And who can blame them? They live in the real world with their office jobs and nuclear families and a host of mindless sitcoms waiting on the propaganda box at the end of their busy day. In direct contrast, it could be observed that anyone who has dedicated themselves to the pursuit of forbidden knowledge really doesn't live in that world at all. Not for lack of wanting, perhaps, but because the real world is quickly seen to be little more than a series of programs and illusions – not unlike The Matrix. And not surprisingly, the people who populate that world may begin to take on a peculiar zombie-like quality.

You find yourself alone in a world of jesters, jokers and jackasses. Now what?

FROM THE AUTHOR
www.quantumshaman.com

ON AMAZON
http://www.amazon.com/Scrawls-Walls-Soul-Della-Hise-ebook/dp/B008CUKH6C/

Eye Scry Publications
A Visionary Publishing Company
www.eyescrypublications.com

www.ingramcontent.com/pod-product-compliance
Lightning Source LLC
Chambersburg PA
CBHW052137170626
46812CB00004B/1473